PUFFIN BOOKS · *Editor: K...*

MY FIRST BIG STORY

All parents ought to read alou... none can make too early a s... world of folk-tale and fairy story. This wonderful world unites the story-teller and his audience in a common experience, where the simple words and phrases which the child can understand fall quite naturally into place. It is, of course, much better if you can tell stories spontaneously in your own words. If you cannot do this, however, read these tales aloud to your children.

I have taken some care to simplify their form and style in order to make them suitable for the earliest years of reading, without in any way reducing or alter- ing their content. I have attempted to retain the simple, natural forms of expression which belong to the primitive folk-tale, and to avoid the kind of polish- ing which results in a 'literary' style. The use of lan- guage which is straightforward and pithy helps to bring the story-teller and his audience together. By listening to such stories, the child gains some inkling of the treasure which the greater world of literature holds in store for him.

I should like to acknowledge my great debt to my wife Maria for all the help she has given me in reading and selecting these stories.

RICHARD BAMBERGER

Cover illustration by Laszlo Acs

Richard Bamberger

My First Big Story Book

Translated by James Thin

Illustrated by Emanuela Wallenta

Penguin Books

Penguin Books Ltd, Harmondsworth, Middlesex, England
Penguin Books Australia Ltd, Ringwood, Victoria, Australia

First published in Austria under the title *Mein erstes grosses Märchenbuch*
English translation published in Great Britain by Oliver & Boyd 1965
This selection published in Puffin Books 1969
Reprinted 1970

Copyright © Verlag für Jugend und Volk, 1960
Translation copyright © Oliver & Boyd, 1965

Made and printed in Great Britain by
Hazell Watson & Viney Ltd, Aylesbury, Bucks
Set in Linotype Pilgrim

Contents

The Turnip

An old man sowed a turnip seed. The rain fell, the sun shone, and the seed grew and grew into an enormous turnip.

One evening the old man thought he would like to have the turnip for supper, so he put on his big boots and went into the field to pull it up. He seized it by the leaves and he pulled and he pulled, but he could not pull it up.

He called to his wife, and she came and pulled the man, and the man pulled the turnip; and they pulled and they pulled, but they could not pull it up.

The little boy came running up, and he pulled the woman, and the woman pulled the man, and the man pulled the turnip; and they pulled and they pulled, but they could not pull it up.

The dog came up with a bark, and took hold of the little boy. The dog pulled the boy, and the boy pulled the woman, and the woman pulled the man, and the man pulled the turnip; and they pulled and they pulled, but they could not pull it up.

Then the hen came with a flutter of her wings, and grabbed the dog's tail with her beak. The hen pulled the dog, and the dog pulled the boy, and the boy pulled the woman, and the woman pulled the man, and the man pulled the turnip; and they pulled and they pulled, but they could not pull it up.

The cock came strutting up. The cock pulled the hen, and the hen pulled the dog, and the dog pulled the boy, and the boy pulled the woman, and the woman pulled the man, and the man pulled the turnip. They pulled and they pulled and they pulled – and up came the turnip, and down they all fell, flat on the ground.

So they all had turnip for supper, and there was plenty left over for the next day and for the day after that.

The Duckling's Journey

A duckling waddled proudly along as he set off on his journey into the wide world.

Along came a frog, who said, 'Where are you going, little duck?'

'I'm going into the wide world!' said the duckling.

'May I come with you?' asked the frog.

'Just sit on my tail,' replied the duckling.

So the frog perched himself on the duckling's tail, and off they went.

By and by they met a pebble, who asked, 'Where are you going, duckling and frog?'

'We are going into the wide world!' replied the duckling and the frog together.

'May I come with you?' asked the pebble.

'Just jump on to my back,' replied the frog.

So the pebble perched himself on the frog's back and off they went.

Soon they met a live coal, glowing red, who said, 'Where are you going, duckling, frog and pebble?'

'We are going into the wide world!' replied the duckling, the frog and the pebble.

'May I come with you, duckling, frog and pebble?' asked the red-hot coal.

'Just jump on to my back,' replied the pebble.

So the red-hot coal perched himself on top, overjoyed that he could see so much of the wide world. On they went together, until they came to a river.

The duckling swam into the water, and when he reached the middle of the river he said, 'Now just a moment, while I dive down to see if I can catch a fish.'

Alas, that was the end of the pebble and the coal. They fell into the water, and they were never seen again.

But the duckling and the frog were quite happy, for they could swim. They laughed till they split their sides, and they are still laughing to this very day.

But people who do not know this story say that they are just quacking and croaking.

The Story of the Five Toes

Do you know why the big toe is so thick, and all the other toes are so thin? Listen, and I will tell you.

The smallest toe went out into the forest one day to look for firewood. The second toe caught a hare, the third toe brought it back home, the fourth one cooked it, and the nasty horrid big toe ate it all himself.

Was that fair? Of course not, and that is why the four little toes keep apart from the big toe to this very day.

The Farmer who Went to Plough

There was once an old farmer who went out to plough his field. He ploughed for a long, long time, and at last his plough turned up a great wooden chest.

'What can be in it?' he wondered. He would have liked to know, but the chest was fastened with an enormous lock. So he went to fetch a locksmith, who had a great many keys. The locksmith tried the biggest key. It fitted exactly, and he opened the chest. What did they see?

Inside the chest there was another chest. The locksmith took the next key, and opened it.

Inside there was a wooden box, and inside the wooden box there was another wooden box, and inside that there was yet another, and so on, and so on. And each time the locksmith had a key that fitted.

At last they came to a tiny box made of gold, but the locksmith had no key small enough to fit it. So he took out a golden pin, and made a little key out of it, and opened the little golden box.

And what do you think was in it? I cannot tell you, for the old farmer and the locksmith kept it a close secret, and no one knows to this very day *what* they found in the little golden box.

The Three Little Pigs

There was once an old woman who had three little pigs who ate and ate and ate, until they had eaten her almost out of house and home.

When they had become so fat that they could hardly fit into their sty, the old woman said to them, 'You cannot stay here any longer. You must go and build your own houses.' And she sent them out into the wide world.

Before long the first little pig met a man with a bundle of straw, and said to him, 'Please, sir, give me the straw so that I can build myself a house.'

'Give me some of your bristles,' said the man, 'so that I can make a brush.'

So the little pig gave him some bristles, and the man gave him the straw and helped him to build a house, with a big door at the front, and a little door at the back. When it was finished, the little pig looked at his house, and sang:

> 'My house is of straw
> And there I shall hide.
> If the big wolf comes,
> I'll be safe inside.'

The second little pig met a man carrying a bundle of wood, and said to him, 'Please, sir, give me the wood so that I can build myself a house.'

'Give me some of your bristles,' said the man, 'so that I can make a brush.'

So the little pig gave him some bristles, and the man gave him the wood and helped him to build a house, with a big door at the front, and a little door at the back. When it was finished, the little pig looked at his house, and sang:

> 'My house is of wood
> And there I shall hide,
> If the big wolf comes,
> I'll be safe inside.'

The third little pig met a man pushing a cart full of stones, and said to him, 'Please, sir, give me the stones, so that I can build myself a house.'

'Give me some of your bristles,' said the man, 'so that I can make a brush.'

So the little pig gave him as many bristles as he wanted, and the man gave him the stones and helped him to build a house, with a big door at the front, and a little door at the back. When it was finished, the little pig looked at his house and sang:

> 'My house is of stone
> And there I shall hide,
> If the big wolf comes,
> I'll be safe inside.'

So each of the three little pigs lived in his own house, and felt quite safe and sound.

But one day the wolf came out of the forest. He knocked at the door of the house of straw and called, 'Little pig, little pig, let me in, let me in!'

But the little pig replied, 'No, no, no, I will not let you in.'

And the wolf said, 'Then I'll huff and I'll puff and I'll blow your house down.'

And he huffed, and he puffed, and the house came tumbling down. But the little pig was nowhere to be found, for he had escaped through the little door at the back. He ran to take refuge with the second little pig, who lived in the wooden house.

So the wolf went to the wooden house, knocked at the front door, and called, 'Little pig, little pig, let me in, let me in!'

But the second little pig replied, 'No, no, no, I will not let you in.'

And the wolf said, 'Then I'll huff, and I'll puff, and I'll blow your house down.'

And he huffed, and he puffed, and the house came tumbling down. But the two little pigs were nowhere to be found, for they had escaped through the little door at the

back. They ran to take refuge with the third little pig, who lived in the stone house.

So the wolf went to the stone house and knocked at the front door, and called, 'Little pig, little pig, let me in, let me in!'

But the third little pig replied, 'No, no, no, I will not let you in.'

And the wolf said, 'Then I'll huff, and I'll puff and I'll blow your house down.'

And he huffed, and he puffed, and he puffed, and he huffed, but no matter how hard he tried, he could not blow the house down.

The wolf became very angry indeed, and said, 'Just you wait! I'll soon find a way to reach you.' And he started to climb up on to the roof, for he meant to come down the chimney.

Now when the three little pigs heard the wolf climbing up and guessed what he had in mind, the first little pig said, 'What shall we do now?'

The second little pig said, 'I shall light a big fire in the fireplace.'

And the third pig said, 'And I shall hang a great cauldron of water over the big fire.'

Not long afterwards, when the fire was crackling merrily – and the water boiling away, the big bad wolf came sliding down the chimney, and landed splash! right in the middle of the boiling water. Quick as lightning the little pigs put the lid on the pot. Then they danced with joy around the hearth singing, 'The wolf is dead, the wolf is dead. Hurrah, hurrah, hurrah!'

So the first little pig built himself a house of stone, and so did the second, and they all lived happily ever after.

The Little Round Pot

There was once an old woman who was very poor and had nothing left to eat. She looked in all her boxes and all her drawers, on all her shelves and in all her cupboards, until at last she found a little flour. She tipped it into a little round pot and cooked some soup with it. When she had eaten it, she washed the pot and laid it on the window-sill to dry, saying, 'Now I shall certainly starve to death, unless God helps me.' Sadly she sat down in her rocking-chair and fell asleep.

The sun shone on the little round pot and dried it, and the pot said, 'Now I must be on my way.'

'Where are you going to, little round pot?' asked the sun.

'I am going to the market-place, to get some food for the poor old woman.' And the little pot bounced down from the window-sill, and off into the town to the market-place, where it rolled about amongst all the people.

Along came a farmer who was carrying a sackful of beans, and he did not know what to do with them. 'Little round pot,' he said, 'you have come just at the right time.' And he emptied all the beans into its little round body.

As soon as the little round pot noticed that it was full again, it said, 'Now I must be on my way.' So it turned round and rolled back to the old woman. It thumped on the door and cried, 'Open up, open up! It is the little round pot!'

The old woman awoke, went to the door and opened it. She looked at the pot, and she was overjoyed when she saw the beautiful juicy beans in its little round body. She cooked herself some bean soup with them, washed the pot till it was spotless, and laid it on the window-sill to dry, thinking, 'God has helped me once – perhaps he will do so again!' Whereupon she fell asleep.

Once again the sun came out and dried the little round pot, and again it said, 'Now I must be on my way to the town, to get some food for the poor old woman.'

It bounced down from the window-sill, and off into the town. It rolled into a butcher's shop, and bounced up on to the counter. The butcher's wife was standing there with a ladle full of beef broth in her hand, not knowing what to do with it. 'You have come just at the right time!' she cried when she saw the little pot, and she poured the broth into its little round body.

The little pot noticed that it was warm and full. It bounced down from the counter, and rolled back to the old woman. Once again it thumped on the door, and cried, 'Open up, open up! It is the little round pot!'

The old woman was indeed delighted. She opened the door, lifted up the little pot, and drank all the warm broth. As before, she washed the little round pot till it was spotless, and laid it on the window-sill to dry.

Once again the sun came out and dried the little round pot, and once again it said, 'Now I must be on my way.'

'Pot, little pot, where are you going to now?'' asked the sun.

'I am going to a rich man, to get some money for the poor old woman.'

So the little pot rolled along to a rich man's house and right up into his room, where he was busy counting his money at the table. He was just thinking that he had more money than he knew what to do with when he saw the little round pot, and he said, 'You have come just at the right time!' And he shook in as many gold pieces as the little round pot would hold.

As soon as the little round pot noticed that it was full, it bounced down from the table, out of the door and down the stairs, bump, bump, bump.

'Come back! Come back!' shouted the rich man, but the little round pot had already disappeared round the corner of the street.

The pot thumped at the old woman's door, and called, 'Open up, open up! It is the little round pot!'

The woman hurried to open the door, and her eyes nearly popped out of her head at the sight of so much gold. She hardly gave herself time to shake it out and to wash the pot, and then, rather than waste time laying it out to dry on the window-sill, she pushed it out of the door, crying, 'Hurry, little round pot, hurry back and bring me more.'

The little round pot was very angry, and it grumbled, 'Very well, very well, I'll be on my way.' But instead of going to the rich man, it rolled along into the town until it came to a halt where some workmen were mending the road. There it waited until it was full of pebbles, and then it rolled back to the old woman. It thumped on the door, saying, 'Open up, open up! It is the little round pot!''

The woman had been waiting at the door, but as soon as she saw what was in the little round pot, she grew very angry, and threw it right out of the window.

The little round pot rolled along into the wide world, and it never came back to the old woman. As far as I know it is still going. Perhaps you will meet it some day.

The Story of the
Thick Fat Pancake

There once was a mother who had seven hungry children. She took flour, milk, butter, eggs, sugar—not forgetting just a pinch of salt—and made a beautiful thick fat pancake. It lay in the pan, and it swelled up until it was a joy to see. The seven children stood round about, and the grandfather looked over the mother's shoulder.

'Mother, dear Mother, please give me the pancake,' said the first child.

'Dear, kind Mother,' said the second, 'please give it to me.'

'Dear, kind, beautiful Mother,' said the third, 'please give it to me.'

'Dear, kind, beautiful, good Mother,' said the fourth, 'please give it to me.'

'Dear, kind, beautiful, good, sweet Mother,' said the fifth, 'please give it to me.'

'Dear, kind, beautiful, good, sweet, wonderful Mother,' said the sixth, 'please give it to me.'

'Dear, kind, beautiful, good, sweet, wonderful, marvellous Mother,' said the seventh, 'please give it to me.'

But Mother replied, 'Wait till it is turned.'

Hardly had the words left her mouth than the pancake began to think, 'I should turn over, should I? But I

am far too beautiful to be eaten. I think I shall go out into the wide world and seek my fortune!'

So it leapt out of the pan and scuttled across the floor, hoppity-hop, and out of the door.

'Come back!' cried Mother as she ran after it, still clutching the pan and ladle, while Grandfather and all the seven children followed behind her.

They all shouted, 'Come back, come back!' But the pancake bounced hoppity-hop downstairs and out into the street.

There it met a cat, and when the cat saw the fine thick fat pancake, she said, 'Miaow, miaow, thick fat pancake, please let *me* eat you!'

But the pancake said, 'What! Shall I be eaten by you, little cat? Mother couldn't catch me, Grandfather couldn't catch me, seven squalling children couldn't catch me; and do you think I can't escape you too?'

And it ran, hoppity, hoppity, hoppity, along the street.

By and by along came a cock, who said, 'Dear thick fat pancake, please let *me* eat you!'

'What!' said the pancake. 'Shall I be eaten by you, little cock? Mother couldn't catch me, Grandfather couldn't catch me, seven squalling children and the cat couldn't catch me; and do you think I can't escape you too?'

And it ran, hoppity, hoppity, hoppity, on into the wide world.

By and by it met a goose, who said, 'Clackety, clackety clack, fat pancake, let *me* eat you!'

'What!' said the pancake. 'Shall I be eaten by you, little goose? Mother couldn't catch me, Grandfather couldn't catch me, seven squalling children and the cat and the cock couldn't catch me; and do you think I can't escape you too?'

And it ran, hoppity, hoppity, faster than ever into the wide world.

By and by along came a cow, who said, 'Moo, moo, thick fat pancake, let *me* eat you!'

'What!' said the pancake once again. 'Shall I be eaten by you, little cow? Mother couldn't catch me, Grandfather couldn't catch me, seven squalling children and the cat and the cock and the goose couldn't catch me; and do you think I can't escape you too?'

And it ran, hoppity, hoppity, hoppity, faster than ever into the wide world.

Along came two little children, a boy and a girl. They were very hungry because they had had nothing to eat all day long. When they saw the thick fat pancake, they cried, 'Pancake, dear pancake, do let *us* eat you!'

But the pancake replied: 'What! Shall I be eaten by you, little Johnny-Jenny? Mother couldn't catch me, Grandfather couldn't catch me, seven squalling children and the cat and the cock and the goose and the cow couldn't catch me; and do you think I can't escape you too?'

And it ran, hoppity, hoppity, hoppity, faster than ever into the wide world.

Along came a pig, who said, 'Come here, thick fat pancake, and let *me* eat you!'

'What!' said the pancake once again. 'Shall I be eaten by you, little pig? Mother couldn't catch me, Grandfather couldn't catch me, seven squalling children and the cat and the cock and the goose and the cow and little Johnny-Jenny couldn't catch me; and do you think I can't escape you too?'

And it ran, hoppity, hoppity, hoppity, faster than ever into the wide world.

But then the pancake came to a brook, and it did not know how to cross over to the other side, for there was no bridge. It ran hoppity, hoppity along the bank, looking for a way to get across.

Now the pig threw itself into the water and swam downstream after the pancake. But the pancake was afraid of getting wet, so the pig said, 'Would you like me to carry you across, thick fat pancake?'

'Yes, please,' said the pancake.

'Then jump on to my back, or better still, on to my snout,' said the pig.

So the pancake leapt on to the pig's snout, but hardly had it landed there when snap! the pig bit it in half, and swallowed one half without delay; but the other half leapt on to the other bank, and scuttled away, hoppity, hop. The pig grunted, and snuffled along after it, but never caught it.

And that is why pigs always snuffle with their snout on the ground, because they are all still hoping to find the other half of the thick fat pancake.

Why the Bear Has a Stumpy Tail

A bear once met a fox, who was slinking by with some fishes, which he had stolen.

'Where did you get them from?' asked the bear.

'I caught them,' replied the fox.

The bear thought that he would like to learn how to fish, and asked the fox to teach him.

'It's really quite easy,' said the fox. 'All you have to do is bore a hole through the ice, and let your tail down into the water. But you must keep it in the water for a very long time, and you must not worry if it begins to hurt a little, for that is a sign that the fish are biting. The longer you stay there, the more fish you will collect. But when you feel a violent nip on your tail, then you must pull it out as quickly as possible.'

The bear followed these instructions carefully, and kept his tail so long in the hole that it was frozen into the ice. When at last he stood up, he left his tail behind, stuck fast! And that is why bears to this very day have stumpy tails.

Porridge

There was once a poor but good little girl, who lived alone with her mother, and they had nothing left to eat. The little girl went out into the forest, where she met a wrinkled old woman, who gave her a little pot, and told her that whenever she was hungry she must say to the pot, 'Cook, little pot,' and the pot would cook some fine steaming porridge. When there was enough porridge, she was to say, 'Enough, little pot,' and it would stop cooking.

The little girl took the pot home to her mother, and they were not hungry any longer, but ate fine steaming porridge as often as they wanted.

One day when the little girl was out, her mother said, 'Cook, little pot.' The pot cooked the most delicious porridge, and she had plenty to eat, but she had forgotten the words to stop it, so the pot cooked on and on till it overflowed. Soon the steaming porridge filled the kitchen, and the whole house, then the next-door house, and then the whole street, until it looked as though the whole world was going to be filled with porridge.

No one knew what to do, and everyone was frantic. At last, when only one house in the town was still clear of porridge, the little girl came back and said, 'Enough, little pot.' And the pot stopped cooking.

But anyone who wanted to go into the city had to eat his way there.

The Three Butterflies

There were once three butterflies, a white one, a red one, and a yellow one, who played in the sunshine, and danced now on this flower, now on that flower, and were so happy that they never grew tired. One day it started to rain and they got wet, so they tried to fly home; but the door was shut, and they could find no shelter, so they had to stay out in the rain getting wetter and wetter.

So they flew over to the lily, and said, 'Good Lily, open your flower a little for us, so that we may shelter from the rain.'

'I shall be glad to take in the white one,' said the lily, 'for he looks like me, but I cannot take in the other two!'

'If you will not take in my friends,' replied the white one, 'I shall stay wet, rather than desert them.'

The rain fell more and more heavily, so they flew across to the tulip and said, 'Dear Tulip, open your flower a little for us, and let us in to shelter from the rain.'

'I shall be glad to welcome the red and the yellow ones,' replied the tulip, 'but cannot take in the white one.'

'If you cannot take in our friend,' said the red and

yellow butterflies, 'then we shall have to do without your help.' And so they flew away together.

But the sun, who was hiding behind a cloud, had overheard them, and it was glad that the three butterflies stood by each other so nobly. It chased the clouds and the rain away, and beamed down on the garden and dried the butterflies' wings. So they danced and played among the flowers for the rest of the day.

The Fly and the Bee

A fly and a bee lived together. One day they were brewing beer in an eggshell, when the fly fell in and was drowned. Thereupon the bee began to cry.

'Why are you crying, Bee?' asked the door.

'Because Fly is drowned.'

Then the door began to creak, and a broom in the corner asked, 'Why are you creaking, Door?'

'Why should I not creak?' said the door.
'Fly is drowned,
Bee is crying.'
Then the broom began to sweep, until a little pram trundled across the floor, and asked, 'Why are you sweeping, Broom?'
'Why should I not sweep?' said the broom.
'Fly is drowned,
Bee is crying,
Door is creaking.'
'Then I must roll,' said the pram, and it began to roll, till it came to the rubbish-heap, which asked, 'Why are you rolling, Pram?'
'Why should I not roll?' said the pram.
'Fly is drowned,
Bee is crying,
Door is creaking,
Broom is sweeping.'
'Then I shall burn,' said the rubbish-heap, and it began forthwith to burn with a bright flame.
A tree was standing nearby, and asked, 'Why are you burning, Rubbish-heap?'
'Why should I not burn?' said the rubbish-heap.
'Fly is drowned,
Bee is crying,
Door is creaking.
Broom is sweeping,
Pram is rolling.'
'Then I must shake myself,' said the tree, and it began to shake itself till all the leaves fell to the ground.
A little girl, who was carrying a jug to the fountain, saw this and asked, 'Why are you shaking, Tree?'

'Why should I not shake?' said the tree.

'Fly is drowned,
Bee is crying,
Door is creaking,
Broom is sweeping,
Pram is rolling,
Rubbish-heap is burning.'

'Then I shall break my jug,' said the little girl, and she broke it.

Then the fountain asked, 'Why have you broken your jug, little girl?'

'Why should I not break my jug?' said the little girl.

'Fly is drowned,
Bee is crying,
Door is creaking,
Broom is sweeping,
Pram is rolling,
Rubbish-heap is burning,
Tree is shaking.'

'Then I must begin to flow,' said the fountain, and it began to gush forth water. And the water washed everything away—the little girl, the tree, the rubbish-heap, the pram, the broom, the door, the bee and the fly.

The Story of the Five Fingers

Micki (the index finger), Licki (the middle finger), Kiki (the ring finger) and little Picki (the little finger) wanted to go for a walk together without their elder brother, big Tocki (the thumb). Tocki warned them, saying, 'Don't go out without me. You will come to no good!' But they paid no attention and set out on their walk.

'I shall show you the way,' said Micki.

'I shall be in charge of you,' said Licki, the biggest of them.

'I shall bring back the treasures we find,' said Kiki.

'And I shall give you good counsel,' said little Picki.

So on they went, Micki in front, then Licki, then Kiki (wearing the ring), and finally little Picki at the rear.

Before long they came to a river where the bridge had been washed away. The water flowed on and on and showed no signs of stopping.

'You are the tallest of us,' said little Picki to Licki. 'Go along the river-bank and see if you can find any way across. Meanwhile, we will build a boat.'

So the three little ones went to look for wood to build a boat, and they found a big walnut.

'If we can only split it in half,' said little Picki, 'we shall have a boat without much trouble.'

So Micki and Kiki seized the nut, one on each side, and pulled with all their might, until the nut split open. Then they hollowed it out, and dragged the shell to the river.

By this time Licki had returned, saying, 'No way across, as far as I can see!'

'No need,' said little Picki, and they all settled down in the nutshell. Little Picki steered, the others rowed, and they soon reached the other side without mishap.

On they went, and before long they came to a big garden, in which they found a huge pot full of honey. Micki clambered up and reached into the pot, and because the honey tasted so sweet, he reached further and further in.

The others were annoyed at this, for they wanted to continue with their walk, but in vain Licki ordered him to come out and show them the way. Kiki was afraid of robbers, and little Picki said, 'If Micki will not show us the way, we shall come to grief.'

All at once they saw a huge bear towering over them. In a voice like thunder, the bear growled,

'Now I have caught you, you thieves! No more honey for you. I'm going to gobble you all up!'

The poor little fellows were so terrified that to begin with they could hardly utter a sound, but at last they all fell down in front of the bear, and pleaded, 'Please, Mr Bear, don't eat us up! We did not know that the garden belonged to you.'

But the bear paid no attention. He was just about to gobble them all up, when little Picki had a bright idea.

'Dear Mr Bear,' he said, 'you only see four of us here, but our fifth brother, Tocki, is still at home. If you can wait for a little while, I will run home and fetch him. Then you will have all five of us for your meal.'

The bear was delighted to hear that he was going to have still more to eat.

As fast as he could little Picki ran home, and shouted, 'Quickly, Tocki, come at once! The bear is going to gobble us up!'

'Did I not tell you not to go out without me?' grumbled Tocki. But he seized an immense club and went with little Picki, and when they reached the honey-garden, they crept up quietly behind the bear, and Tocki killed him with a single blow of his club.

From that time onwards the four fingers never went out without Tocki, and no harm has ever come to them.

Licki has always remained in the middle, and big Tocki and little Picki go as scouts at either side. Tocki defends them all by his strength, and little Picki by his quick wits.

Cock and Hen in the Wood

Cock and Hen once went to the wood to eat nuts. A nutshell stuck in Hen's throat, and she lay gasping and choking. Cock ran to the well to fetch some water for Hen, saying, 'Well, well, give me some water. I must take the water to Hen, who has swallowed a nutshell and is lying choking in the wood.'

But the well answered, 'I can give you no water till you give me some leaves.'

So Cock ran to the lime tree. 'Lime tree, lime tree, give me some leaves. I must take the leaves to the well, then the well will give me water, and I must take the water to Hen, who has swallowed a nutshell and is lying choking in the wood.'

'I can give you no leaves till you give me a gold bangle,' replied the lime tree.

So Cock ran to the princess. 'Princess, princess, give me a gold bangle. I must take the bangle to the lime tree, then the lime tree will give me leaves, and I must take the leaves to the well, then the well will give me water, and I must take the water to Hen, who has swallowed a nutshell and is lying choking in the wood.'

'I can give you no gold bangle till you give me a pair of shoes,' replied the princess.

So Cock ran to the cobbler. 'Cobbler, cobbler, give me

a pair of shoes. I must take the shoes to the princess, then the princess will give me a gold bangle, and I must take the bangle to the lime tree, then the lime tree will give me leaves, and I must take the leaves to the well, then the well will give me water, and I must take the water to Hen, who has swallowed a nutshell and is lying choking in the wood.'

'I can give you no shoes till you give me some bristles,' replied the cobbler.

So Cock ran to the pig. 'Pig, pig, give me some bristles. I must take the bristles to the cobbler, then the cobbler will give me shoes, and I must take the shoes to the princess, then the princess will give me a gold bangle, and I must take the bangle to the lime tree, then the lime tree will give me leaves, and I must take the leaves to the well, then the well will give me water, and I must take the water to Hen, who has swallowed a nutshell and is lying choking in the wood.'

'I can give you no bristles till you give me some corn,' replied the pig.

So Cock ran to the thresher. 'Thresher, thresher, give me some corn. I must take the corn to the pig, then the pig will give me some bristles, and I must take the bristles to the cobbler, then the cobbler will give me shoes, and I must take the shoes to the princess, then the princess will give me a gold bangle, and I must take the bangle to the lime tree, then the lime tree will give me some leaves, and I must take the leaves to the well, then the well will give me water, and I must take the water to Hen, who has swallowed a nutshell and is lying choking in the wood.'

'I cannot give you any corn till you give me some bread,' replied the thresher.

So Cock ran to the baker. 'Baker, baker, give me some bread. I must take the bread to the thresher, then the thresher will give me some corn, and I must take the corn to the pig, then the pig will give me some bristles, and I must take the bristles to the cobbler, then the cobbler will give me shoes, and I must take the shoes to the princess, then the princess will give me a gold bangle, and I must take the bangle to the lime tree, then the lime tree will give me leaves, and I must take the leaves to the well, then the well will give me water, and I must take the water to Hen, who has swallowed a nutshell and is lying choking in the wood.'

The baker was sorry for poor Cock, and gave him bread. So the thresher got his bread, the pig its corn, the cobbler his bristles, the princess her shoes, the lime tree its gold bangle, the well its leaves, and Cock his water. Cock took the water to Hen, who was still lying and gasping in the wood, choking on a nutshell, and Hen got better again.

Rag, Tag and Bobtail

'The nuts are ripe now,' said Rag the cock to Tag the hen. 'Let's go up on to the hill and have a feast, before the squirrels get them all.'

'Delighted,' said Tag the hen. 'Let's go and make gluttons of ourselves.'

So off they went up the hill, and stayed there till evening.

Now I do not know whether it was because they had eaten so much, or just because they were growing uppish, but they simply refused to walk home, so Rag the cock made a fine little coach out of nutshells.

When it was ready, Tag the hen sat down inside it, and said to the cock, 'Now, dear Rag, harness yourself!'

But Rag would do nothing of the sort. 'I would sooner walk home,' he said, 'than allow myself to be harnessed. I don't mind being a coachman, but I will *not* be a horse!'

While they were quarrelling thus, Bobtail the duck came rushing down the hill at them, angrily quacking, 'You thieves, who gave you permission to eat nuts in *my* wood? Just you wait.' And with wide-open beak and flapping wings, she flew at Rag the cock.

But Rag was ready for the attack, and struck back vigorously. He hacked away with his spurs at the poor duck, until she begged for mercy, and allowed herself to

37

be harnessed to the coach as a punishment. Rag stood in front on the driving seat as the coachman.

Bobtail took the bit in her bill and pulled with all her might. The nutshell coach with its two plump passengers was almost too heavy for her to move, but at the third strong pull away went the coach down the hill, with Bobtail running in front as fast as her flat webbed feet would carry her.

When they had gone some distance they met two travellers, a darning needle and a sewing needle, who cried, 'Stop, stop! Take us with you! It will soon be pitch dark, and it is so muddy on the track that we can go no further. We have run away from the tailor's shop by the town gate, and we are looking for shelter for the night.'

They were thin folk, who took up little room, so they were allowed into the coach, but they had to promise not to prick Rag and Tag.

Late at night they came to an inn, and as Bobtail the

duck was rather shaky on her feet, they decided to stay there. To begin with the innkeeper did not want to have them, but Rag the cock promised, 'You shall have the egg which Tag laid on the way here, and you can keep Bob-tail the duck, who lays an egg every day.'

So the innkeeper let them in, and they ordered an enormous meal.

Early next morning, while it was still dark and every-one was asleep, Rag wakened Tag, and they ate the egg between them, leaving the egg-shell on the hearth. Then Rag took the two needles, who were still sleeping, and stuck one of them in the innkeeper's cushion and the other in his towel; and off he flew with Tag across the fields without saying a word to anyone.

Bobtail the duck was sleeping outside in the courtyard, but she was wakened by the sound of Rag and Tag flying past, so she plunged quickly into the stream and swam happily away.

A few hours later the innkeeper awoke. He washed his face and dried it on his towel, but the darning needle scratched across his face, and left a great red streak from one ear to the other. Then he went into the kitchen to light his pipe, and when he came to the hearth he saw the empty egg-shell lying there.

'Nothing seems to be going right this morning,' he grumbled, and sat down in his big armchair. But he quickly leapt up again, crying 'Ouch!' for the sewing needle had stuck deep into him.

By now he was angry, and suspected the visitors who had come so late the previous evening, but when he went to look for them, he found they had flown. So he swore that never again would he take such rag, tag and bobtail into his inn, to eat too much, to pay for nothing, and to play nasty tricks into the bargain.

The Magic Horse

There once lived a rich merchant who had a fine big garden behind his house, as well as a piece of land which he had planted with corn. One day, while he was strolling in his garden, he noticed that someone had been taking his corn. He resolved to catch the thief and have him punished. He called his three sons, Michael, George and John, and said, 'There was a thief in my field last night, and he has taken a great deal of my corn. I want you, my sons, to take turns in keeping watch at night. Whoever catches the thief shall be richly rewarded.'

The first night Michael, the eldest son, kept watch. He took pistols and a sharp sword with him, as well as food and drink, wrapped himself in a warm overcoat and settled down under a lilac tree. Soon, however, he was fast asleep, and when he woke up next day he saw that still more of the corn had been taken.

The next evening it was George's turn to keep watch. He also took pistols and a sword with him, together with a stout cudgel and a length of rope. But this good watchman fell asleep like the first, and next morning he found that the thief had been hard at work again.

The third night it was John's turn. He took neither pistols nor sword with him, but gathered a ring of thorns and thistles round about himself. Every time he started to nod the thorns pricked his nose, and he was wide awake instantly. Towards midnight he heard a clippety-clop, clippety-clop, faintly in the distance to begin with, then closer and closer till he could hear it in the field in front of him . . . clippety-clop, clippety-clop.

Quietly John gathered up his rope, pushed the thorns and thistles aside, and crept silently forward. He saw a charming little horse! It allowed John to catch it without difficulty, and it followed him to the stable of its own accord.

Early next morning his brothers woke him. They laughed at him and made fun of him. 'A fine watchman you are!' they taunted. 'You did not even stick to your post through the night!'

So John took his father and his brothers to the stable, where the wonderful horse stood, and no one knew where it had come from or to whom it belonged. It was finely built, and silvery white all over. The father was delighted, and gave it as a reward to John, who called it Corn-robber.

Some time after this the three brothers heard of a beautiful princess who lived, under a magic spell, in a castle on a mountain made of glass. The approach to the castle was so highly polished and so slippery that no one could reach it, but it was said that whoever could ride up to the castle without mishap, and then ride three times round about it, would thus release the princess from the magic spell and win her as his bride. Many young men had already made the attempt, but they had all slipped and fallen, and they lay dead at the foot of the glass mountain.

The three brothers thought they would like to try their luck. Michael and George bought beautiful and powerful steeds, and had them shod with specially sharp horse-shoes, but John saddled his little Corn-robber, and off they set together.

Before long they reached the foot of the glass mountain. The eldest was first to make the attempt, but before he had gone far his horse slipped, and both horse and rider fell to the foot of the mountain, where they both lay still. The same thing happened to George, and both horse and rider came crashing to the bottom and lay where they had fallen. Then John set off up the mountain, clippety-clop, clippety-clop. The horse's hooves rang out cheerfully on the glass, and before long they were at the summit. On they went, clippety-clop, just as if Corn-robber had trotted the same way many times before.

John dismounted at the massive castle door, and it opened to reveal the most beautiful princess he had ever seen, dressed from head to foot in silk and gold. Full of joy she welcomed him and embraced him. Then she turned to the pony, and said, 'You little scoundrel, running away from me like that! I was allowed an hour's freedom each night, when I could visit the green earth down below, but without you I was unable to get there at all. You must never leave us again!' So John realized that his Corn-robber was the princess's magic pony.

It was not long before his two brothers recovered from their fall, but John never saw them again, for he lived happily with his bride in the magic castle on the glass mountain.

King Adder

A long, long, time ago a poor girl was servant to a farmer, who was very hard on her. At first cock-crow she had to jump out of bed, and go into the cowshed to milk the cows, and she worked hard early till late.

One morning, while she was milking the cows, she

heard a small rustling sound in the straw on the floor, and looking down she saw a snake with a golden crown on its head gliding between her feet. At first the girl was petrified with fear, but she saw the adder eyeing the bucket hopefully, so she plucked up her courage and dipped the bucket down to let it drink.

It must have been very thirsty, for there was only a dribble of milk left in the bottom of the bucket when it had finished drinking. The poor girl took the bucket to the farmer's wife in fear and trembling, expecting a severe scolding. But to her astonishment, so much milk flowed out of the bucket that three large bowls were filled instead of the usual one, and even the farmer's sour-faced wife smiled at her.

From that day onwards the adder came to her every morning and every evening to drink milk. Whenever it had drunk, it gave the girl such a look of trust and gratitude that she forgot all her troubles and was filled with joy. Things continued in this way for a number of years, until the girl grew, and became the most beautiful girl in the whole village, so that all the young men were in love with her. She fell in love with a young farmer and promised to marry him.

At last came her wedding day. The dishes were steaming, the musicians were playing, and all the guests were making merry.

When the feast was at its height, an uncanny silence settled over the room, for the adder was seen gliding across the floor, straight for the bride and bridegroom. It slithered up the back of the bride's chair and on to her right shoulder, and shook the golden crown off its head on to the empty plate. Then it glided away and disappeared for ever.

The bride took this glittering souvenir and put it in her purse. From that day forth her purse always had plenty of money in it, no matter how much she spent, so that she became the richest and most respected farmer's wife in the whole district.

The Mouse, the Bird and the Sausage

Once upon a time a mouse, a bird and a sausage lived in the same house. They shared the work, and for a long time they lived happily together. Every day the bird flew into the forest to collect firewood, the mouse brought the water, made the fire and set the table, and the sausage did the cooking.

One day this bird met another bird, and told it all about the fine life with the mouse and the sausage. But the other bird said, 'You poor fool! You are wearing yourself away doing all the hard work, while the other two just sit at home and enjoy themselves. For the mouse, as soon as she has brought the water and lit the fire, lies down for a little nap, until it is time to set the table. The sausage just watches the pot to see that everything is all right, and when it is nearly dinner-time, he just rolls himself once or twice through the broth or vegetables, and they are buttered, salted and cooked.'

As soon as the bird came home and laid down his burden, they took their places at the table, and when the meal was over they lay down and slept till the following morning. What a splendid life!

But the next day the bird refused to fetch any more wood. 'I have been a slave for long enough,' he said. 'We must change round and have turn and turn about.'

The mouse and the sausage did their best to persuade the bird, but he would not give way. They drew lots to decide which work each must do, and from now on the sausage was to fetch the wood, the mouse was to do the cooking, and the bird was to fetch water.

What happened?

The sausage went out for wood, the bird laid the fire, and the mouse stayed and watched the pot. They waited for the sausage to come home with the wood, but he was such a long time away that they were afraid something had happened to him. So the bird flew out to look for him.

Not far away he found a dog, who had seized the poor sausage and swallowed him. The bird scolded the dog angrily, but that did not help to bring the sausage back again.

Sorrowfully the bird picked up the wood, and flew home to tell the mouse the sad story. They were very downhearted, but decided to stay together, just the two of them.

So the bird set the table for two, while the mouse climbed into the pot, as she had seen the sausage do, to stir up the vegetables. But alas, she was boiled alive.

When the bird came to put the food on the table, he

found no cook there. In distress he threw the wood on the floor, called and shouted, and looked all over the place, but no cook was to be found. Because of his carelessness the wood caught fire, and the bird ran to fetch water. As he leant over the well to let down the bucket, he fell in and was drowned.

If you are well off, don't be discontented and start looking for something better.

The Straw, the Coal and the Bean

An old woman had just enough beans left to cook a single meal. She lit the fire, and heaped on a big handful of straw, so that it would burn up more quickly; and she emptied the beans into the pan. But one bean fell out on to the hearth and came to rest beside a piece of straw. A lump of red-hot coal jumped out of the fire, and landed beside them.

'Dear friends,' said the straw, 'where have you come from?'

'Luckily I was able to escape from the fire,' replied the coal, 'or I should have been burnt to ashes.'

'I also was fortunate to escape with a whole skin,' said the bean. 'I should have been cooked to a pulp like my comrades, if the old woman had managed to put me in the pan.'

'I should certainly have fared no better,' said the straw. 'The old woman sent all my brothers up the chimney in smoke – sixty of us were seized and thrown mercilessly into the fire. I alone managed to escape.'

'What ought we to do?' asked the coal.

'We have all escaped disaster,' said the bean. 'I propose that we should stick together, and go out into the world to seek our fortunes.'

This proposal suited the other two very well, so off they set. But soon they came to a small stream. There was no bridge and they were unable to cross over.

Suddenly the straw had a bright idea, and said, 'I will lie across the stream, and you two can walk over me.'

So he stretched himself from one bank to the other. The coal was a brave young fellow and he stepped boldly on to the bridge. Half-way across, however, when he saw the water rushing and foaming beneath him, he grew afraid and came to a halt. He was still red-hot and he burnt through the middle of the straw, which broke in two, so that they both fell into the stream and were drowned.

This set the bean laughing, and he laughed so long and loud that he split his sides. Now this would have been the end of him, had a tailor not been passing that way. The tailor took pity on the poor bean, and with needle and thread from his pocket he sewed up the slit. He only had black thread with him, and so from that day to this all beans have had a black seam down their sides.

The Servant Lass

A mother had seven sons, who were far away, and a little daughter, who lived with her at home.

As the girl grew older, people used to say to her, 'How lucky you are, having seven brothers!'

So she went to her mother one day, and said, 'Mother, have I *really* seven brothers?'

And the mother said, 'Of course you have, but they are living a long way from home.'

'Let me take our servant lass,' said the girl, 'and go to look for my brothers.'

So her mother sent her forth with the servant lass. The daughter rode on horseback and the servant lass sat behind her.

When they had gone some distance they came to a spring. The sun was hot and the girl was very thirsty, so she jumped from her horse, and went for a drink of water. While she was drinking, the servant lass took hold of the horse's reins and rode off, leaving the poor girl to follow on foot.

When they came to the place where the seven brothers lived, the young men took the servant lass for her mistress, and left their real sister to look after the poultry.

The servant lass was given a golden chair to sit on, and a golden apple to play with, but the real sister was left to weep amidst the geese and the hens.

Before long, however, the brothers discovered how the servant lass had tricked them. They put their true sister in the golden chair, and gave her the golden apple to play with. But the servant lass was beaten soundly, and put out of doors to look after the geese and the hens.

Wild Rose

A very long time ago there lived a king and queen, who used to sigh every day and say, 'If only we had a child!' But the years went by, and no child came.

Then one day, when the queen was bathing, a frog hopped out of the pool and spoke to her.

'Your wish will be fulfilled,' it said. 'Within a year you will bring a daughter into the world.'

And so it happened. The queen had a baby daughter, who was so lovely to look at that the king was beside himself with joy, and gave a great banquet to celebrate.

He invited not only friends and relations, but also the Wise Women, for he wanted them to be well-disposed towards the child. There were thirteen of these Wise Women in the kingdom, but as he had only twelve golden plates left, he asked only twelve of them.

The banquet was truly magnificent. When it was over, the Wise Women bestowed their magic gifts on the baby, who had been called Wild Rose. One gave her beauty, another virtue, a third wealth, and so on, until the baby had everything that might be desired in the world.

When eleven of them had announced their gifts, the thirteenth came in, furious that she had not been invited to the banquet, and eager to avenge herself of the insult. Without a word of greeting, without looking to right or left, she pointed at the baby and cried, 'The princess shall prick herself on a spindle in her fifteenth year, and shall fall down dead!' So saying, she turned on her heel and left the room.

Everyone was dismayed, but the twelfth Wise Woman, who had not yet bestowed her gift, stepped forward. She could not cancel the evil promise, but she could at least soften it. 'The princess will not die, but she will sleep for a hundred years,' she said.

Now the king wanted to safeguard Wild Rose, so he ordered that all the spindles in the kingdom were to be burnt. In the meantime, all the good gifts of the Wise Women showed themselves in the princess, who grew up beautiful, gentle, polite and friendly, so that everyone was fond of her.

Now it happened that on the princess's fifteenth birthday the king and queen were away from home, and she was left alone in the castle. She wandered about through all the rooms, and came at last to an old tower. She climbed a narrow spiral staircase, and at the very top she found a little door, with an old rusty key in the keyhole. As the key grated in the lock the door sprang open, and

there in a tiny little room sat an old woman at her spinning wheel, busily spinning a fine flaxen thread.

'Good-day,' said Wild Rose. 'What are you doing?'

'I am spinning,' said the old woman, with a nod.

'What is that strange-looking thing, that turns round so merrily?' said the princess, stretching out her hand to feel it. But as she touched the spindle, she pricked her finger and the magic spell was fulfilled.

At the very moment when she felt the prick, she fell into a deep sleep. And this sleep spread itself throughout the castle. The king and queen, who had just returned, fell asleep with their whole court in the great hall. The horses slept in the stables, the dogs slept in the courtyard, the doves slept on the roof, and the flies slept on the walls; even the fire, which was flickering away merrily on the hearth, died down, and the roast meat on the spits stopped sizzling. The cook, who was pulling the scullery-boy's hair because he had forgotten something, let him go, and the kitchen-maid, who was plucking a black chicken, let go of the handful of feathers she was about to pull. Everybody slept. Even the wind died down, so that there was not the faintest breeze to flutter the leaves on the trees which grew in the castle gardens.

All round the castle a hedge of thorns began to grow. Year after year, it grew higher and higher, until at last it completely surrounded the castle, and not even the flag on the topmost tower could be seen from the other side.

The story of the beautiful Wild Rose spread far and wide, and from time to time kings' sons would come to try to find a way through the hedge into the castle. But none succeeded, for the thorns clung closely together as if they had hands, and the young men became entangled in them and could not escape.

After many a long year, a king's son came into the country and heard from an old man the story of the hedge of thorns, of the castle inside, and of the beautiful princess called Wild Rose, who, together with the king and queen and the whole court, had been sleeping for a hundred years. He had already heard from his grandfather how a great many princes had tried to cut a way through the thorns and had come to grief, but he was determined to try his luck. 'I am not afraid!' he said. 'I will go and see this beautiful Wild Rose for myself.'

The hundred years had now passed by, and it was time for Wild Rose to wake up again, so when the prince approached the hedge of thorns, he found nothing but flowers, which parted of their own accord to let him through unharmed, then gently closed again behind him. In the courtyard he saw the dappled hounds and the horses in the stables, all lying asleep. The doves sat on the roof with their heads tucked under their wings, and when he went inside, he found the flies still asleep on the walls, the cook's hand outstretched towards the scullery-boy, and the maid, fast asleep, clutching the black hen which she had been plucking.

On went the prince, and found the whole court lying asleep in the great hall, with the king and queen asleep on their thrones. On he went, with everything so still that he could hear himself breathe, until he came to the tower with the spiral staircase and the little door, which led into the attic room where Wild Rose lay sleeping.

She was so beautiful as she lay there that he could not take his eyes from her, and he bent down to give her a kiss. No sooner had he kissed her, than Wild Rose opened her eyes and smiled sweetly up at him.

They went downstairs hand in hand, and the king and queen, with the court, woke up. The horses in the stables stirred and shook themselves; the hounds in the courtyard leaped up and wagged their tails; the doves on the roof pulled their heads from under their wings, blinked and flew off to the woods; the flies crawled up the walls, the fire burst into flame, and the roast meat on the spits began to sizzle; the cook gave the scullery-boy a box on the ear, and the maid finished plucking the black hen.

The prince and Wild Rose were married and they lived happily ever after.

Beauty and the Beast

Once upon a time there lived a merchant who travelled a great deal in foreign parts. Once, as he was saying good-bye to his three daughters, he said, 'My dear daughters, what would you like me to bring home for you?'

'Dearest Father,' said the eldest, 'please bring me a beautiful pearl necklace.'

'I should like a sparkling diamond ring,' said the middle one.

But the youngest one whispered shyly, 'Father, please bring me a green hazel twig, as a sign that you have not forgotten me.'

So the merchant set off on his travels. His affairs prospered, and he did not forget his daughters. He packed the pearl necklace and the diamond ring in his bag, but no matter how hard he searched, he was unable to find a green hazel twig.

He was still distressed about this when, on his way home, he came to a dark forest. As the track led through the thick undergrowth, he felt something brush against his face. There was a sound like hailstones falling to the ground, and when he looked up he saw a beautiful green hazel twig, with golden nuts hanging on it. He was overjoyed, and stretched up his hand to break it off.

At that very moment a huge bear shot out of the undergrowth, uncovering its fangs in a dreadful snarl. It towered up on its hind legs as if about to rend the merchant limb from limb, and roared, 'Why have you broken my hazel twig?'

'Dear bear,' said the merchant, quivering with fear, 'let me take the hazel twig and go home in peace, and I will send you an enormous ham, and as many sausages as you can eat.'

'Keep your ham, and your sausages,' bellowed the bear. 'You may go only if you promise to give me the first living creature that comes to meet you when you return home.'

The merchant promised. He felt sure that his dog would be the first creature to come running to him, and he did not mind sacrificing the dog in order to save his own life.

So the bear padded off into the forest and the merchant continued his homeward journey, with the golden hazel twig glittering in his hat. To his horror, as he approached his house, he saw his youngest daughter running to meet him, while the dog stood on the doorstep behind her. In great distress he told his family what had happened when he broke the hazel twig, and they were filled with dread.

A few days later a black carriage drew up in front of

the house, and out of it stepped the ugly great bear. With a growl and a snarl he padded into the house, and there he insisted that the father should keep his promise. There was no help for it, and the poor girl had to go. Sad at heart she said good-bye, and off she went in the carriage with her horrible bridegroom.

Once outside, the bear laid his shaggy head in the girl's lap, and growled, 'Stroke my head, scratch my ears and tickle my chin – or I will eat you.'

The girl stroked and scratched him so gently that the bear was delighted. The carriage flew along more swiftly than the wind, and it seemed as though the black horses had grown wings. Soon they came to the dark forest and the carriage came to a halt at the entrance to a cave. This was the bear's dwelling. How terrified the girl was when she saw the black cave gaping among the rocks! Nor was her terror any the less when the bear clasped her round the waist with his huge hairy arm, and whispered gently, 'Here you are to live and be content; but you must do what I tell you, or my wild beasts will eat you.'

They stepped forward into the cave. The bear pushed open a massive iron gate, and they entered a room which was full of poisonous snakes, whose tongues darted out towards them. The bear growled into his bride's ear, 'Take great care to look neither to right nor to left – then you will be safe.'

The girl passed through the room looking neither to right nor to left, and no snake touched her. And so they passed on to the next room, and again, as they crossed the threshold, the bear growled, 'Look neither to right nor to left – then you will be safe!' In this way they passed through ten rooms, and the eleventh room was full of all the most horrible of monsters – dragons, poisonous toads and serpents. Again the bear growled, 'Look neither to right nor to left – then you will be safe!'

The girl trembled with fear, but she remained steadfast,

and looked neither to right nor to left, and passed safely through the eleventh room.

So they reached the twelfth room, and there a brilliant light gleamed through the open door, and the girl could hear music, and sounds of joy and great jubilation. There came a clap of thunder, and then deep silence.

In that clap of thunder forest, cave, monsters, bear – all vanished. Before her rose a splendid castle, crowned with turrets of gold, with a host of servants standing to welcome her at the gate; and at her side, instead of the huge, growling bear, stood a young man, a prince, tall and handsome. He joyfully kissed his bride, thanking her for releasing him, through her courage, from the spell which had bound him. The hazel twig had been the key to her good fortune.

Her father and her sisters were invited to the castle for the wedding. The prince and his bride were married, and they all lived happily ever after.

The Man who Kept House

There was once a man who was always grumbling and dissatisfied. Never could his wife work hard enough, or do anything right in the house.

One evening at harvest-time he came home late from the fields, and at once began to scold and to find fault with his wife, so that it was quite dreadful to hear him.

'Don't be so bad-tempered, you old ninny,' said his wife. 'Tomorrow we will change places. I will go out into the fields with the harvesters, and you shall do the house-work.'

That suited him very well, so early next morning the woman laid the scythe over her shoulder and went off to the fields with the harvesters, while the man stayed at home.

To begin with he thought he would churn some butter, so he filled the butter-tub with cream and churned for a while. But soon he felt thirsty, so he went down to the cellar to fetch a jug of beer. He pulled the bung out of the barrel, and let the beer run into the jug.

Suddenly he heard a pig scampering around in the kitchen overhead, so he raced upstairs at once with the bung still in his hand, for he was afraid that the pig might upset the butter-tub.

He was too late, however; the tub lay on its side, and the pig was busy lapping up the cream, which was running all over the floor. This put him in a rage and he chased the pig across the room, and felled it with a blow.

He then realized that he was still clasping the bung in his hand, so he rushed down to the cellar, only to find that all the beer had flowed away, and the barrel was empty.

Back he went to the dairy, and once more filled the butter-tub with cream, which he proceeded to churn, for he wanted butter for his lunch. After he had been stirring for a while, he realized that the cow had been left in the cowshed, without anything to eat or drink.

It was too late now to drive her out to pasture, but he thought he would put her on the roof, which had a thick covering of fine rich grass. The house lay on a steep slope, and he thought he would lay a plank from the hillside on to the roof, so that he could bring the cow across.

But he did not want to leave the butter-tub lying in the kitchen, for his little boy was crawling around the floor and might easily upset it, so he took it on his back and out he went.

Before leading the cow on to the roof, he wanted to give her a drink. He took a bucket and filled it at the spring, but as he bent down all the cream poured out of the butter-tub, down his neck and into the water.

It was now almost lunch-time. He had had no luck with the butter, so he thought he would cook some gruel. He filled a big pot with water and hung it over the fire. Then it occurred to him that the cow might fall off the roof and break her leg, or even her neck, so he took a rope, went up on to the roof, and tied one end of it round the cow's neck. He threw the other end down the chimney, returned to the kitchen, and fastened the rope round his own leg.

The milk was just beginning to boil, so he began to stir in the oatmeal, but suddenly the cow fell off the roof, and jerked the man halfway up the chimney on the end of the rope. There he hung, able to move neither up nor down, while the cow hung down in front of the house, suspended between heaven and earth.

The good wife waited and waited for her husband to bring her lunch, but there was no sign of him. Eventually she grew tired of waiting, and went home to see what was happening.

There she saw the cow hanging between heaven and earth, so she reached up and cut the rope with her scythe, and the cow landed happily on four legs. But the man fell down the chimney, and when the woman went into the kitchen she found him standing on his head in the pot of gruel with his legs waving in the air.

The Shepherd and the Dwarf

A great many years ago there lived a poor shepherd who had seven sheep, which he grazed on a high mountain slope. One day he was leaning on his crook and thinking of his children at home, for times were hard, and he was very poor.

Speaking quietly to himself, he murmured, 'My poor children, if only I could give you enough to eat every day!'

Scarcely had the words left his lips when a little dwarf stood before him, with a red cap and a long straggly beard. 'Come with me,' said the dwarf, 'and I will show you something worth seeing.' So the shepherd followed him.

Now the dwarf was holding a root in his hand, and the shepherd went after him until he came to a halt at the foot of a steep cliff. Three times he raised the root and struck the rock, and it split open with a clap of thunder, revealing a deep dark cave. The dwarf stepped inside, followed by the shepherd.

At the back of the cave burnt a fire, where many sooty-faced dwarfs were at work, forging all sorts of costly and beautiful things out of gold – crowns and chains, rings and bowls, cups and bangles. The shepherd's eyes almost popped out of his head at the sight of so much gold. 'Take as much as you want,' said the dwarf, 'but don't forget the most important thing of all.' So saying, he laid the root on the ground and vanished.

The shepherd had no need to be told twice, but stuffed all his pockets with gold and set off home. The moment he set foot outside the cave, the rocks clapped together with another peal of thunder.

The gold enabled the poor shepherd to buy food and shoes and clothing for his children for some time, but at last these good times came to an end. Day after day he wandered up and down the cliff face looking for the entrance to the cave, but the mountain remained closed for ever, for he had forgotten the most important thing of all – the magic root!

The Three Goats called Hurricane

There once lived three goats, who set out to graze on the hillside. All three were called Hurricane.

On the way to the pasture there was a bridge over a

river, and under the bridge lived a horrible great troll with eyes as big as saucers, and a nose as long as a broomstick.

The first goat came trotting along, and wanted to cross. Clippety-clop, clippety-clop he clattered on to the bridge.

'Who's that trotting on my bridge?' boomed the troll.

'It is I, the little goat Hurricane,' replied the goat in his small high voice. 'I am going up the hillside to graze.'

'Just you wait, I'm coming up to catch you!' boomed the troll.

'I shouldn't waste time catching me,' said the goat. 'I am still very small. Just wait a few moments for the other goat Hurricane. He is much bigger than I am!'

'All right,' boomed the troll.

Not long afterwards the second goat came trotting along and wanted to cross. Clippety-clop, clippety-clop he clattered on to the bridge.

'Who's that trotting on my bridge?' boomed the troll.

'It is I, the second goat Hurricane,' replied the goat, in his stronger, deeper voice. 'I am going up the hillside to graze.'

'Just you wait, I'm coming up to catch you!' boomed the troll.

'Oh, I shouldn't bother about me,' said the goat. 'Why not wait for the big goat Hurricane? He is much bigger than I am!'

'All right,' boomed the troll.

By and by along came the big goat. Bonk! bonk! bonk! bonk! he tramped on to the bridge.

'Who's that tramping on my bridge?' boomed the troll.

'It is I, the big goat Hurricane,' replied the goat in the strongest, deepest voice.

'So it's you at last,' boomed the troll. 'I'm coming up to catch you!'

'Come along then,' replied the big goat Hurricane. 'I have two fine spears on my head, and it won't take me long to deal with a fat old ugly brute like you!'

So the goat lowered his horns and hurled himself at the troll. He battered him with his hooves and tossed him into the river. Then he went to join the other two on the hillside.

And the three goats ate so much that they grew fatter and fatter, until they could hardly move. If they have not burst yet, I suppose they must still be eating.

The Wolf and the Seven Kids

There was once an old goat, who had seven kids whom she loved dearly, as a mother loves her children. One day when she was going into the forest to look for food, she called her seven kids to her and said: 'My dear children, be on your guard against the wicked wolf while I am away in the forest, and lock the door. If he should get into the house, he will certainly gobble you all up. The villain often disguises himself, but you will easily be able to recognize him by his black paws and his gruff voice.'

'Dearest Mother,' said the kids, 'we will take great care; there is no need to worry about us.' So the mother goat bleated good-bye, and trotted cheerfully away; and the kids locked the door.

Not long afterwards there was a knocking at the door, and a voice called, 'Open the door, dear children. It is your mother, and I have brought home something for each of you.'

But the kids heard the gruff voice, and they knew that it was the wolf. 'We will *not* open the door,' they shouted. 'You are not our mother, for she has a soft gentle voice, and your voice is gruff. You are the wolf.'

So the wolf went to a shop and bought a big stick of chalk, which he swallowed, in order to soften his voice. Back he went and knocked again at the door, calling, 'Open the door, dear children. It is your mother, and I have brought home something for each of you.' But the wolf had laid his black paws on the window-sill, and the kids saw them and called back, 'We will *not* open the door. You are not our mother, for her feet are not black. You are the wolf.'

So the wolf went to the baker's shop and said, 'I have hurt my paw. Please plaster some dough on it.' When the baker had done this, the wolf ran off to the miller and said, 'Please powder my paw with flour.'

Now the miller suspected that the wolf intended to deceive someone, and he refused, but the wolf said, 'If you don't do what I tell you, I'll gobble you up.' So the miller was afraid, and powdered the wolf's paw with flour.

For the third time the scoundrel went to the house and knocked on the door, saying, 'Open the door, dear children. It is your mother home again, and I have brought something for each of you from the forest.'

'Show us your foot,' cried the kids, 'so that we may tell if you are really our mother.'

So the wolf laid his paw on the window-sill, and they saw how white it was and thought it really was their mother, so they unlocked the door.

In came the wolf! The kids were terrified, and tried to hide. One dashed under the table, one under the bed-clothes, the third into the oven, the fourth into a drawer, the fifth into a cupboard, the sixth under a basin, and the seventh inside the grandfather clock. But the wolf found them and gobbled them up one after the other – all except the youngest one, who was hiding inside the grandfather clock. When the wolf had finished his meal, he trotted outside, sauntered across the meadow, and lay down beneath a tree to sleep.

By and by the mother goat came home from the forest. What a shock it was to her to see the door standing open, tables, chairs, and benches thrown all over the place, dishes smashed to smithereens, blankets and pillows dragged off the bed! She looked for her children, but they were nowhere to be found. She called them one after the other by name, but no one answered, until she came to the youngest of all. Then she heard a faint voice calling, 'Here I am, Mother, in the grandfather clock.' So she pulled him out, and the little fellow told her the sad story of how the wolf had gobbled up all his brothers and sisters. You can imagine how she wept for her poor children!

In her grief she left the house, and the youngest little kid ran along beside her. When they came to the meadow they found the wolf lying under a tree, snoring so loudly that the branches were quivering. She examined the wolf from all sides, and saw that something was moving and struggling in his great fat stomach. 'Good gracious!' she said. 'Can it be possible that my poor children are still living?'

So she sent the little kid home for scissors, needle and

thread, and when he returned she quickly cut open the wolf's stomach. Hardly had she made the first cut when one little kid thrust his head out, and with each cut another little kid appeared, until all six of them were jumping and skipping round her. They had not come to the slightest harm, for the wolf in his greed had swallowed them whole. What rejoicing there was, as they kissed their dear mother and skipped about for joy!

'Run and fetch me some big stones,' said the mother goat, 'so that I can fill the scoundrel's stomach while he lies sleeping.' So the seven kids ran quickly and brought seven stones, each as big as themselves, and stuffed them into the wolf's stomach. Quick as thought the mother goat sewed the stomach up again, but very gently, so that the wolf did not even stir in his sleep.

When at last the wolf did wake up, he dragged himself to his feet, and went to look for a drink because the stones inside had made him thirsty. But the stones bumped against each other and rattled when he began to walk, so that he cried out, 'Whatever is this fearful rattling and bumping going on inside me? I thought it was six tender little kids I had eaten but it feels more like six great boulders!'

He struggled over to the well and bent down to drink, but the weight of the seven stones pulled him in and he was drowned. When the seven kids saw this they came running up, crying at the top of their voices, 'The wolf is dead! The wolf is dead!' And they danced round the well for joy.

The Fox as Shepherd

A farmer's widow went to look for someone to take care of her animals. On the way she met a bear.

'Where are you going?' asked the bear.

'I'm going to look for a shepherd,' replied the woman.

'I'll look after your animals for you,' said the bear.

'How will you call them to come to you?' asked the woman.

'Gr-r-r-r-r,' growled the bear.

'No, that won't do at all,' said the woman, and she went on her way.

By and by she met a wolf. 'Where are you going?' asked the wolf.

'I'm going to look for a shepherd,' replied the woman.

'I'll look after your animals for you,' said the wolf.

'How will you call them to come to you?' asked the woman.

'Uhoohoohoohooooo!' howled the wolf.

'No, that won't do,' said the woman, and she went on.

Not long after that she met a fox. 'Where are you going?' asked the fox.

'I'm going to look for a shepherd,' replied the woman.

'I'll look after your animals for you,' said the fox.

'How will you call them to come to you?' asked the woman.

'Dil-dal-hollow, dil-dal-hollow,' sang the fox, in a fine, deep, tuneful voice.

'That will do very well,' said the woman, and she engaged the fox on the spot to take care of her animals.

On the first day, when the fox was taking the animals

out to the meadow, he gobbled up all the goats; on the second day he made a good tasty meal of sheep; on the third day it was the cows' turn. When he came home in the evening, the woman asked him where he had left all the animals.

'Oh, they are out there on the banks of the stream and in among the bushes,' said the fox. Now the woman was standing by her butter-tub churning cream to make butter, but when she heard this she stepped outside to have a look for her animals. While her back was turned, the fox stuck his head into the butter-tub and gobbled up all the cream. The woman was furious, chased him with her cream whisk, and hit him on the tip of his tail as he ran away.

And that is why the fox has a white tip to his tail to this day.

The Cock and the Neighbour's Hen

A man had a cock who could do all sorts of clever tricks, and the woman next door had a hen, who tried to imitate this cock in everything he did. Now one day the man said to his cock, 'Fly away and bring me money – plenty of it!'

So off flew the cock, straight to the palace, where he perched on the canopy above the emperor's bed, and crowed loudly:

'Cock-a-doodle-doo!

Fi! Fi! Fi!

The emperor is a lazy loon.

He stays in bed till afternoon!'

The emperor was furious, and ordered his footmen to

lock the shameless bird up in the barn. But the cock ate all the grain, flew out of a hole in the roof, and once again perched on the canopy above the emperor's bed, crowing more loudly than ever.

'Cock-a-doodle-doo!

Fi! Fi! Fi!

The emperor is a lazy loon.

He stays in bed till afternoon!'

The emperor was purple with rage, and ordered his footmen to shut the impertinent bird in the Copper Treasury. But the cock gobbled up all the copper, flew back to the emperor's bed, and crowed again. Thereupon he was locked in the Silver Treasury, where he gobbled up all the silver. Then he flew back to the emperor's bed and crowed again. Thereupon he was locked in the Gold Treasury. The cock gobbled up all the gold, and flew off home.

On the way home he dropped a penny, which fell into a puddle. When he saw his master's house in the distance, he crowed, 'Spread out all your cloths and sacks, I'm coming!' So the man made haste to spread out all the cloths he had, and scarcely had he done this when the cock

flew up and filled them all with grain, copper, silver and gold.

The woman next door was extremely envious, for she also would have liked to become rich in such an easy manner. So she asked her neighbour how he had trained his cock to bring him so many fine things.

'I just gave him a good beating,' said the man.

So the woman gave her poor hen a sound beating, and said, 'Off you go, and bring me as much money as the neighbour's cock brought him!'

'All right,' replied the hen, 'I won't be long.' Off she flew until she came to the puddle where the cock had dropped the penny. This pleased her greatly, and she lapped it all up – puddle and penny and dirt and all. Back she waddled, weighed down with all she had swallowed, and from far off she squawked to her good woman: 'Spread out all your cloths and sacks, I'm coming!'

Quick as lightning the woman spread out all the cloths

which she had made ready, but the hen filled them all with puddle water and dirt and the single penny.

The cock noticed the penny, gobbled it up, and cried, 'That one is mine – you are welcome to the rest!'

Never again did the hen try to imitate the neighbour's cock.

The Bremen Town Musicians

A man had a donkey, who for many a long year had carried his sacks to the mill. But now the donkey was growing old and was not fit for work, so his master thought that the poor animal was no longer worth his keep. The donkey well realized that his master held no good intentions towards him, so he ran away on the road to Bremen.

Before he had gone far he met a dog lying panting by the roadside.

'What's the matter with you, old fellow?' asked the donkey.

'Alas!' said the dog, ' I am growing old and weak, and cannot hunt any longer for my master. He wanted to kill me, so I ran away from home, but how I am going to earn my food is more than I can guess.'

'Now you listen to me,' said the donkey. 'I am going to

Bremen to join the town band. Why not come with me, and try your hand at music? I'll play the lute, and you can beat the drum.' The dog thought this was an excellent idea, so off they went together towards Bremen.

Before long they met a cat sitting by the wayside, with a face as long as three rainy days.

'What's worrying you, old whiskers?' asked the donkey.

'How can I look happy,' replied the cat, 'when my life is in danger? I am old, my teeth are no longer sharp, and I prefer to lie in front of the fire rather than to hunt mice. My mistress thinks I am not worth my keep. She wanted to drown me, so I ran away. But where can I go?'

'Come along with us to Bremen! You know all about serenading, so you can become a town musician with us.'

This suited the cat very well, so off she went with the dog and the donkey. By and by they came to a farm-yard, where the cock was perched on the gate, crowing with all his might.

'You are making enough noise to waken the dead!' said the donkey. 'What's the trouble?'

'Tomorrow is Sunday and we are having guests to dinner,' said the cock. 'The good lady of the house means to have chicken soup, and I am to have my head cut off this very evening. So I am crowing at the top of my voice while there is still breath left in me.'

'But why not come along with us, red-comb!' said the donkey. 'We are going to Bremen to be town musicians, and you have a fine powerful voice.' So the cock fell in with this plan, and all four of them went on together.

But they were unable to reach Bremen in one day, and as it grew dark they came to a wood, and there they proposed to spend the night. The donkey and the dog curled up beneath a great tree and the cat climbed on to a branch overhead, while the cock perched himself to roost on the very tip of the tree, where he felt quite safe from danger.

Before settling down he took a good look round, and saw a light in the distance; so he called down to his companions, 'There must be a house not far off, for I see a light.'

'Let's go and have a look,' said the donkey, 'for I have known better places than this for a night's rest.'

The dog felt that a good bone with some meat on it would not go amiss, so off they set in the direction of the light, which soon grew brighter and bigger, until they came to the house from where it was shining out. The donkey was the tallest, so he crept up to the window and peeped inside.

'What do you see, old fellow?' asked the cock.

'What do I see?' replied the donkey. 'I see a table set with all kinds of good things to eat and drink, with four robbers sitting at it and having a gay old time.'

'We could do with some of that,' sighed the dog.

'Yes, if only we could get in,' agreed the donkey.

So they put their heads together, and worked out a plan for chasing the robbers away, and this is what they did. The donkey stood with his fore-feet on the window sill, the dog jumped on to the donkey's back, the cat climbed on top of the dog, and the cock perched on top of the cat's head.

Then at an agreed signal, they blared out their music together: the donkey brayed, the dog howled, the cat miaowed, and the cock crowed 'Cock-a-doodle-doo!' After that they burst through the window, sending broken glass flying in all directions.

At this frightful clamour the robbers leapt to their feet, having little doubt that a ghost was amongst them, and dashed out in terror into the forest. So our four comrades made themselves at home, and ate and ate as if they had been starving for weeks.

When they had finished eating and drinking, the four

musicians put out the light and sought a place to sleep, each one according to his own taste. The donkey lay down in the midden in the yard, the dog settled himself behind the door, the cat curled up in the hearth, and the cock perched on the rafters overhead. They were tired after their long journey, and soon fell asleep.

Shortly after midnight the robbers saw from some distance off that the light was out, and they felt a little ashamed at having been so easily scared away. Back they went to the house, and found everything quiet. One of the robbers was sent inside into the kitchen to make sure that all was well; not a sound did he hear, so, taking the cat's glowing fiery eyes for two live coals, he stuck a spill into them in order to light it. This was no joke for the cat, who sprang spitting at the robber's face and scratched him. The robber leapt back in terror, but tripped over the dog, who got to his feet and bit the intruder in the leg. As the robber fled through the yard the donkey let fly a powerful kick with his hind-legs. Awakened by all this din, the cock crowed lustily from the rafters: 'Cock-a-doodle-doo!'

The robber fled out to his comrades as fast as his legs would carry him. 'There's a horrible witch in the house,' he gasped, 'who scratched my face with her long fingers. Behind the door stands a man with a sharp knife, who stabbed me in the leg as I passed. In the yard there is a dreadful black monster, who let fly at me with a wooden club, while up on the roof sits the judge, who called out, "Bring the rogue here!" So I took to my heels and ran.'

The robbers made no further attempt to enter the house after that. The four Bremen town musicians made themselves quite comfortable there, and decided to make it their home.

The Princess who Saw Everything in her Kingdom

A beautiful princess lived in a castle and at the top of the topmost tower there was a room with twelve windows. Through each of these windows she could see her kingdom : a little of it from the first window, a little more from the second, more still from the third, and so on. From the twelfth window she saw everything in her kingdom, both above and below the ground.

Now one day she had it announced throughout the land that she would marry the man who could hide himself so well that she would be unable to find him. The lives of the suitors that she found would be forfeit. In rapid succession ninety-seven young men tried their luck and lost their lives in the attempt. For a very long time no one else came forward, and this pleased the princess greatly, for she had no wish for a husband.

At long last three brothers came to see how they would fare. The first one hid in a hole in the ground, but the princess spied him from the very first window, and had him hauled out – and that was the end of him. The second brother hid in the castle cellar, but the princess spied him also through the first window. So he, too, was dragged out and put to death.

Thereupon the youngest of the brothers came before her, saying, 'Dear Princess, allow me a full day to think of a hiding place, and let me off with my life if I fail on the first two attempts. If I fail on the third attempt, I shall willingly lay down my life for you.' Rather to his surprise the princess agreed.

The young man had a whole day in which to consider where he could hide, but no matter how hard he racked his brains, he could not think of anywhere.

For want of anything better to do, he took up his gun and went out into the forest. Before long he saw a raven, took careful aim at it, and was about to pull the trigger when – 'Don't fire!' croaked the raven, 'and I'll see that you are well rewarded.'

So he lowered his gun, and went on his way. Not long after this he came to the bank of a lake, where he saw a huge salmon swimming. He took careful aim, and was about to pull the trigger when – 'Don't fire!' spluttered the salmon, 'and I'll see that you are well rewarded.'

So he lowered his gun and went on his way. By and by he saw a fox, who was limping. He took careful aim and was about to pull the trigger when – 'Don't fire!' barked the fox. 'Rather come here and pull the thorn out of my paw.' So he pulled the thorn out. 'Thank you,' said the fox. 'I'll see that you are well rewarded.'

So the young fellow let the fox go, and as it was growing dark he returned home.

Next day he had to hide himself. He had still no idea where to go, so he ran to the raven in the forest. 'Tell me where to hide myself,' he said, 'where the princess will be unable to find me.' The raven pulled an egg out of his nest. he split the egg carefully in two with his beak, and shut up the young fellow inside it. Then he put the egg back in his nest, and sat down on it.

The princess stepped up to the first window, but nowhere could she see her suitor, nor could she see any sign of him from the second, third and fourth windows, nor from the fifth, sixth, seventh, eighth, ninth and tenth windows. Then at last, when she came to the eleventh window, she saw him. She had the poor raven shot, and ordered the egg to be brought and split open in front of her. 'So,' she said, 'that is your first life gone!'

Next day the young man went to the lake and called the salmon. 'Tell me a good place to hide,' he said, 'where the princess will be unable to find me.' The salmon said it would conceal him in its stomach. So it swallowed him, and dived away down to hide in the reeds at the bottom of the lake.

The princess looked through all the windows in turn, but could not see him anywhere, not even from the eleventh window. She was very worried, and scared at the thought that she might have to take a husband. She stepped up to the twelfth window, and there she saw him. She had the salmon caught and killed and slit open, and the young man had to crawl out. 'That's two lives gone!' she said triumphantly.

Sadly he departed, and on the third and last morning he went into the forest to see the fox. 'Tell me where I can hide,' he said, 'where the princess will be unable to find me.'

'Follow me,' said the fox. They went to a pool, where the fox dived in and was instantly turned into a merchant. 'Now you dive in,' he said. So the young man dived in, and

was instantly turned into the daintiest little guinea-pig.

The merchant took the pretty little animal into the town, and showed it to all the people, who crowded round to look at it. Even the princess came to see it, and was so delighted with it that she bought it for herself. Hastily the merchant whispered to the guinea-pig, 'When the princess goes to the window, creep quickly under her hair.'

The time came for her to look for her suitor. She stepped up to the first window, and saw nothing. She stepped up to the second window and saw nothing. The same thing happened with the third, fourth, fifth, sixth, right up to the eleventh window. She stared out of the twelfth window for a long, long time, but not a sign of him did she see, and in a furious temper she shut this last window so violently that the whole castle shook.

She stepped back, and as she did so she felt the guinea-pig tickling the back of her neck. She flung it to the floor, shouting: 'Away with you! Never let me see you again!'

The little animal scuttled straight back to the merchant, and they both hurried to the magic pool, where they dived in without delay. Once again the merchant was the fox and the guinea-pig was the young man, who thanked the fox for all his help, saying. 'The raven and the salmon were simpletons beside you! You are a genius indeed!' The fox was delighted with this praise, and trotted off happily into the forest.

The young man hurried to the castle to claim his bride. They were married and he became king over the whole kingdom. But he never told his wife where he had hidden on that last occasion. So she thought that he was much more clever than she was, and held him in the greatest respect.

The Fox and the Geese

A fox once came to a meadow where a flock of fine plump geese were sitting. 'I see I have come just at the right time,' he said, laughing. 'You are all sitting so beautifully in a line, that I can gobble you up at my leisure, one after the other.'

The geese cackled loudly in their terror, flapping their wings and screaming, and they begged piteously for their lives. But the fox paid no attention, and said, 'No, this is no time for mercy, you must all die.'

At last one of them plucked up courage. 'If we *must* die,' she said, 'permit us at least one last prayer. When we have finished praying we will wait quietly in a row, so that you can easily choose the plumpest of us.'

'That sounds a reasonable and a pious request,' replied the fox. 'Pray away then, and I will wait till you have finished.'

So the first goose began a long prayer, saying, 'Ga! Ga!' and for ever repeating 'Ga! Ga!' As she did not seem to be near the end of her prayer, the second goose did not wait, but began: 'Ga! Ga!' The third and fourth followed without delay, and soon all the geese were loudly praying together 'Ga! Ga!'

When they have finished their prayer this story can be continued, but at present they are still at it.

The Princess in the Fiery Tower

There was once a poor farmer who had so many children that all the other people in the village were god-parents to them. When his last baby son was born, he sat down by the road-side to ask the first person he saw to be god-father.

By and by an old man came along, wearing a long grey cloak, and leading a cow with her calf on a rope. The old man went with the farmer to assist at the baptism, and made a present of the cow to the poor farmer, and of the calf to his god-son. The calf had been born on the same day as the baby boy, and had a golden star on his brow.

As the boy grew up, he would lead the calf out to pasture day after day, and in time the calf grew into a fine powerful bull. But this bull could speak, and when they came to the hillside he would say to the boy, 'Lie down here and sleep, while I go and seek my own pasture.' So the boy would lie down and sleep.

Meanwhile the bull would run like the wind till he came to the heavenly pasture, where he ate golden sunflowers all day long. When the sun sank in the evenings he would return and wake up the boy, and they would go home together.

Life went on in this way day after day until the boy reached his twentieth birthday. Then one day the bull said to him, 'Sit between my horns, and I will take you to the king. Ask him for a steel sword ten feet long, and say that you are going to set his daughter free.'

In due course the lad stood before the king. 'Your Majesty,' he said, 'give me a steel sword ten feet long, and

I will set your daughter free.' The king gave him the sword, but he had little hope of ever seeing his daughter again, for she had been carried far, far away by a terrible dragon with twelve heads. No one could approach the dragon's lair, for the way there led over a high range of inaccessible mountains, beyond which lay a wide and tempestuous ocean, and the princess herself was shut in a high tower, which was surrounded by a ring of flames. Even if anyone should succeed in crossing the mountain range and the mighty ocean, he would be unable to penetrate the fiery ring round the tower – and even if he should manage to overcome the flames, the dragon would be sure to devour him.

The young fellow gripped the sword, took his place once again between the bull's horns, and in the twinkling of an eye they stood before the great mountain range. 'Now we shall have to go home,' he said to the bull, 'for no one could possibly scale these mighty peaks.'

'Just wait a minute,' said the bull, setting the lad gently on the ground. Then he trotted back a short distance, turned and charged the mountains, pushing the whole range aside with his powerful horns. The youth mounted again, and on they went.

It was not long before they reached the ocean, which was so wide and stormy, with mountainous waves and huge columns of foam, that you would have thought no one could cross it. 'Now we shall have to go home,' said the lad.

'Not so soon!' said the bull. 'Hold fast to my horns!' Then he lowered his fine head and drank the ocean dry, so that they could cross over the ocean bed dry-shod.

Soon they drew near the ring of flames, through which

they could see the tower glowing red in the pall of smoke.
'Hold on,' said the bull, 'or we shall catch fire.' The heat
was terrific, and the sweat was pouring down the lad's
brow, while the bull's coat was already beginning to singe.
He ran as close as he dared to the flames, and coughed up
the ocean which he had swallowed, so that the fire was
extinguished and a dense cloud of mingled smoke and
steam covered the whole sky.

With a blood-curdling screech the twelve-headed
dragon came rushing out of the smoke, all twelve mouths
breathing fire, and all twenty-four eyes sending forth
darts of flame.

'Now it's up to you,' said the bull, 'but you must take
care to hew off all twelve of the monster's heads at one
blow!'

So the lad gathered up all his strength and swung the
sword round his head, and brought it down on the dragon
with such skill and violence that all twelve heads were
severed.

'Now my service is at an end,' said the bull with a sigh. 'Go into the tower and find the princess, and take her home to her father the king.' Saying this, the bull galloped away to the heavenly meadow, and was never seen or heard of again.

The young man went into the tower, and the princess flung herself into his arms, overjoyed to be set free from the wicked dragon. Back they went to the royal palace, where they were married amidst great celebrations.

The Queen Bee

Two brothers once went in search of adventure, and fell into very bad ways. As they did not come home again, their young brother, who was called Simpleton, set out to look for them. When at long last he found them, they laughed at him and made fun of him, saying, 'How on earth do you expect to make your way in the world? We are more intelligent than you, and yet we find the wide world both cruel and difficult.'

All three brothers journeyed on together, and by and by they came to an ant-hill. The two older brothers wanted to churn it up with their feet, and see the thousands of terrified ants rushing round trying to save their eggs. But Simpleton stopped them, saying, 'Leave the little creatures in peace, and do not disturb them.'

Some time after this they came to a lake on which a great many wild ducks were swimming. The two older brothers wanted to catch and roast a few, but Simpleton prevented them, saying, 'Leave them alone, and do not kill them.'

Not much further on they came to an oak tree where there was a nest of wild bees, crammed full of honey. The two older brothers wanted to light a fire round the tree and smoke out the bees, so that they could steal the honey, but Simpleton said, 'Leave the creatures in peace, and do not burn them.'

Now the three brothers came next to a great castle, where the stables were filled with stone horses. It was indeed a strange place, silent as the grave, with no one to be seen. They went through the stables and right at the end they saw a heavy oaken door, fastened by three enormous locks, but there was a peep-hole through which they could see a little grey man sitting at a stone table in the middle of the entrance hall. They called him twice, but he did not stir. They called him a third time, and he stood up and came and unlocked the door with three huge keys which hung on a chain from his belt. The keys grated harshly in the locks, which had clearly not been opened for a long time. Not a word did the little grey man speak, but he beckoned them to follow him to a table heavily laden with good things to eat and drink. After they had eaten, he conducted each to a separate bedroom, comfortably furnished and with everything made ready for them.

Next morning the little grey man came to the eldest brother, and led him to a stone table on which were engraved the three tasks which had to be carried out if the castle was to be delivered from enchantment. The first task was to find the three princesses' thousand pearls, which lay hidden beneath the moss in the forest; but if a single pearl was missing by sunset, the seeker would be turned to stone.

The eldest brother went to the forest and searched all

day long, but when the sun went down behind the trees he had only found a hundred pearls, and he was turned to stone.

The following day it was the second brother's turn, but he did not fare much better. He found only two hundred pearls before the sun went down, and he also was turned to stone.

At last it was Simpleton's turn to look under the moss. But after an hour or so he had found only a few pearls, and

in despair he sat down on a boulder and wept. Along came the king of the ants, with a long procession of five thousand of his subjects behind him, whose lives and home Simpleton had saved earlier. It was not long before these little creatures had found all the thousand pearls, and had dragged them into a little heap.

The second task was to fetch the key of the princesses' bed-chamber from the mud at the bottom of the lake. When Simpleton reached the lake, the ducks whose lives he had saved came swimming to meet him. Before long they had dived down and found the key for him.

The third task was the most difficult of all, for he had to decide which of the three sleeping princesses was the youngest and sweetest. But they all looked exactly alike, and the only way to tell the difference was that just before going to sleep one had eaten a sugar-lump, one had sucked a spoonful of syrup, and the youngest one had taken a little honey.

In flew the queen bee whose nest Simpleton had saved from burning, and hovered gently over the lips of the three sleeping princesses. At last she came to rest on the lips of the one who had eaten honey, and so Simpleton knew which one was the youngest and sweetest.

So the magic spell was broken, and all the stone figures in the castle came to life again. Simpleton married the youngest and sweetest princess, and became king after her father's death, whilst his two brothers married her two sisters.

The Kitten and the Knitting Needles

Once upon a time there was a poor woman who went out into the forest to collect firewood. When she was coming back with her bundle, she saw a sick kitten lying under a bush, moaning piteously. The poor woman lifted it up tenderly and carried it home in her apron.

On the way back she was met by her two children, who saw what she was carrying and asked for the kitten to play with; but she would not give it to them for fear that they might torment it. She laid it down gently at home in a basket of old woollen clothes, and set a saucer of warm milk before it. The kitten lapped up the milk and started to purr, and it was not long before it was quite well again. Then suddenly it disappeared into the forest.

Some days later the woman went once more into the forest to fetch wood, and as she was on the way back with her load she met a tall lady in a long flowing robe standing where the kitten had lain. The lady beckoned to the poor woman, and threw five knitting needles into her apron without saying a word; then suddenly she vanished. The woman did not know what to make of this, but took the knitting needles home and laid them on the table. Next morning, much to her amazement, a fine pair of new socks lay on the table.

Next evening she laid the knitting needles again on the table, and the following morning another pair of new socks lay beside them.

She realized that the magic needles were her reward for having been kind to the kitten. Every night after that the knitting needles were hard at work and the woman sold the socks, so that never again did she lack anything in her little cottage.

The Swan Maiden

One day a young nobleman was out hunting. Suddenly he saw three swans circle overhead and land in a nearby lake. He was astonished to see that the swans laid their feathers (which resembled fine silk dresses) on the grass bank, and appeared swimming in the lake as three lily-white maidens. Shortly afterwards they clad themselves in their feather-mantles again and flew away in the direction from which they had come. But one of them – the youngest and most beautiful – had so bewitched our young nobleman, that, night or day, he could find no peace.

The young man's mother soon noticed that her son no longer took pleasure in hunting or in any other amusement, and she asked what was troubling him. He told her about the three swans, and said that he could never be happy again until the white maiden was his bride.

'Your wish can be fulfilled,' said his mother, who understood these things. 'Go next Thursday at sunset to the

place where you last saw her, and watch carefully where she lays down her feather-mantle. Take it and hurry away with it, and before long you will see two pure white swans fly away, but the third maiden will come to you. But if you want to keep her, on no account let the feather-mantle out of your hands, even if she begs you for it on her knees.'

The young man did exactly as his mother had told him, and before sunrise on the following Thursday he concealed himself in the reeds at the edge of the lake. The sun was sinking low on the horizon, and he did not have long to wait before there was a whirring of white wings overhead, gleaming in the gold of the setting sun, and the three swans glided down on to the bank. They laid their feather-mantles on the grass, and three beautiful maidens skipped over the white sand into the shimmering water.

Softly our young man crept forward, lifted his swan-maiden's feather-mantle, and hid himself in the bushes. Soon afterwards he heard two swans fly away, but the third maiden came to him and threw herself on her snow-white knees before him, imploring him to return her feather-mantle.

'No,' said the young man, and he raised the maiden and covered her with his own cloak. Then he set her in front of him on his horse and took her home, where they were married shortly afterwards.

For many years they lived happily together, and their children were the most lovely creatures who ever played in a castle courtyard.

Seven years passed by, and the happy couple had retired to bed one Thursday evening, when the man took it into his head to tell his wife how he had won her. On her request he brought out the feather-mantle, which he had kept concealed ever since. Scarcely had he laid it in her hands when she changed into a swan, and soared swift as lightning through the window.

The nobleman never saw his wife again.

The Giant and the Tailor

There was once a tailor who was a great boaster. One day he thought he would like to have a look round the country-side, so he left his shop and off he went over bridge and stile, over hills and through valleys, into a part of the country where he had never been before. After some time he thought he saw an enormous tower rising in the dis-tance behind a steep hill.

'Whatever can that be?' wondered the tailor, who was inquisitive by nature; so off he plodded to have a closer look at it. As he drew near, however, the tower suddenly sprouted legs, and turned out to be a huge giant who leapt over the mountain in a single bound and stood looking down on him from a great height.

'What are you wanting here, little midget?' asked the giant, in a voice like thunder, which echoed and re-echoed from the surrounding hills.

'I am just having a look round,' replied the tailor in his thin little voice, 'to see if I can earn an honest piece of bread in the forest.'

'If that's all you want,' thundered the giant, 'you can work as my servant.'

'All right,' squeaked the tailor. 'What wages shall I receive?'

'Wages?' repeated the giant. 'I'll give you three hundred and sixty-five days a year; how does that suit you?'

'Not bad,' replied the tailor, who quietly resolved to escape as soon as the opportunity should present itself.

'Go then, little match-stick,' said the giant, 'and fetch me a jug of water.'

'Perhaps I should bring you the whole spring, and the stream along with it?' suggested the boasting tailor, as he ran off to the well with the jug.

Now the giant was rather a stupid fellow really, in spite of his tremendous size, and he did not understand this sort of joke. 'What's that?' he rumbled in his beard, while the tailor was away. '"The whole spring, and the stream along with it?" I must look after myself, for this fellow is clearly more than he looks – he must possess some strange magic power!'

When the tailor had brought the water, the giant told him to go into the forest and fetch a few sticks of wood for the fire.

'Would it not be better,' said the boasting tailor, 'to chop down the entire forest with a single blow, and take

it home with us? After all, a few small sticks won't keep you warm for long!' And off he went to fetch the wood.

By this time the giant was becoming quite worried. 'The entire forest at a single blow?' he rumbled in his beard. 'And the whole spring, and the stream along with it? I must certainly look after myself, for this midget of a tailor must indeed have some strange power.'

The tailor came plodding wearily back with some sticks, and the giant ordered him to go and shoot two or three wild boars for supper.

'Would it not be better to shoot a thousand with a single shot?' said the boasting tailor. 'I am sure a big fellow like you must enjoy a good hearty appetite!'

'What!' exclaimed the cowardly giant, who by this time was really scared. 'I think you have done enough work for one day – off you go and have a rest.'

Now the giant was so frightened of the little tailor that he hardly had a wink's sleep that night, for lying awake and turning over in his mind how he might rid himself of his confounded serving man, who was undoubtedly a powerful sorcerer in disguise.

Next day the giant and the tailor went to a certain pond, which was surrounded by willow trees. Slyly the giant bent a huge branch down to the ground, and put his foot on the end of it. 'Let's see if you are heavy enough to hold this branch down,' he said to the boasting tailor. So the little fellow sat astride the branch, and no sooner was he comfortably seated than the giant removed his foot and released the branch, hurling the little tailor head over heels so far up into the sky that he disappeared from sight.

And if he has not come back to earth yet, he must still be hovering somewhere overhead.

Cinder Joe becomes King

A long time ago there was a farmer who had three sons. The two older ones were fine strapping young fellows, but proud and envious, while the youngest one was small and delicate, but kind and gentle. The two older boys laughed at him and teased him, never allowed him to play with them, and never took him anywhere with them; they called him Cinder Joe because he was always sitting at home amongst the cinders.

Now it happened that the king died suddenly, and it was announced throughout the realm that everyone was to gather in the royal park one evening at sunset, when it would be decided who was to be the next king. So the two older brothers put on their best clothes and set off for the royal park. Cinder Joe wanted to go with them, but they would not let him.

'We should be thoroughly ashamed of you,' they said. 'Stay at home amongst the cinders – that's where you belong!'

But he followed unseen some distance behind them. When he arrived at the royal park he was afraid his brothers would notice him and send him home, so he crept into a pigsty where no one could see him.

When it was time for choosing a new king, the crown was laid on the top of a little hillock, and all the bells in the palace began to ring. Suddenly the crown rose slowly into the air, hovered high over the heads of the people, and finally sank lower and lower until it came to the pigsty, where it vanished from the watching crowd.

Everyone rushed up to the pigsty to see what had happened, and there they found Cinder Joe with the crown on his head. They carried him outside, and everyone knelt before him and hailed him as the new king who had been called to the throne. Then they carried him in triumph to the palace, but the two proud brothers crept quietly home, too ashamed to show their faces. For it is not important how proud and strong you may be, but rather how good and kind-hearted you are.

The Grateful Snake

There was once a poor woman who could not afford enough bread to feed her only son. So one day the boy went into the forest and gathered firewood, which he took into the town and sold for two pennies.

On the way back he came across a number of boys who were trying to kill a snake. He was sorry for the poor creature, and shouted, 'Stop! If you leave it alone I'll give you a penny!'

So the boys took his penny and let the snake escape, but the snake glided along behind the young fellow, and followed him all the way home. He told his mother what he had done, and she scolded him severely for wasting a penny, but he said, 'Don't be angry, Mother, for the snake was harming no one.'

After they had gone to bed the snake crept quietly into the boy's bed, and whispered, 'You have saved my life, and

I should like to reward you. Get up and dress. We will go to my father and claim a reward. Accept neither money nor gold, but ask for the signet ring which he has hidden away.'

So the boy took the snake back to his father, who was overjoyed to see him alive and well.

'What would you like as a reward?' he asked.

'Neither money nor gold,' replied the boy, 'but rather the signet ring which you have hidden away.'

'I cannot give you what you ask for,' said the father, who had turned quite pale.

The snake turned away as if to depart, so the father, fearful of losing his son again, ran and fetched the signet ring, which he handed to the boy, saying, 'Here is your ring; it will bring you good luck. Whenever you turn it

round on your finger a genie will appear, and he will fulfil all your commands.'

The boy thanked him and took leave of the snake, who wished him good fortune. When he returned home he found his mother worried about what they were going to eat. He said to her, 'Look in the cupboard – you will find plenty to choose from!'

Quick as lightning he turned the ring on his finger, and a genie appeared while his mother was crossing the room to the cupboard. 'Fill the cupboard with food!' he ordered. And when the woman opened the door, she found the cupboard stuffed from top to bottom with all sorts of good things.

From that day forward they led a grand life, lacking neither food nor clothes, nor any of the luxuries of life. But by and by the boy grew bored, and one day he said to his mother, 'Go and tell the king that I want to marry his daughter.'

'What are you thinking of?' said his mother. 'Folk like us don't ask for kings' daughters in marriage!' But he insisted, so she went to the palace and made his request to the king. 'My son would like to marry your daughter,' she said.

'All right,' replied the king with a laugh. 'He may if he can build a palace bigger than this one in a single night!'

The woman returned with this answer to her son. That night he turned the ring on his finger, and when the genie appeared he issued his orders. 'Build me a palace which is bigger than the king's palace!'

Next morning he sent his mother back to the king. 'My son has built a palace which is bigger than yours,' she said, 'so you must give him your daughter.'

But the king tried to escape by saying, 'First he must pave the way from his palace to mine with gold!'

The woman returned and told her son what the king had said, so he turned the ring once again. 'Build me a path of gold,' he said when the genie appeared, 'just as the king has ordered.'

Next day the woman stood before the king a third time.

'My son has paved the way with gold,' she said. 'Give him your daughter as a wife.'

The king could raise no further objections, so the young fellow married the princess, and they lived contentedly together for many a long year.

The Millet Seed

There was once a poor lad whose parents had died, leaving him nothing but a tiny millet seed. As he had nothing else in the whole wide world, he took his millet seed and went out to seek his fortune. Before he had gone far he

met an old man with a grey cloak and a wide-brimmed hat, who smiled at him.

'Good-day to you, sir,' said the lad.

'Good-day to you,' said the man. 'Where are you going?'

'I'm going to seek my fortune,' said the lad, 'and I am carrying my entire worldly wealth with me. It is a millet seed, and I only hope that no one will steal it.'

The man was sorry for the boy, and said, 'I'm afraid you will certainly lose it, but don't worry – you will gain more than you lose.'

That evening the lad came to a village, knocked at a farm door, and asked for shelter for the night. Before he went to sleep, he laid his millet seed on the window sill and said to his host, 'This is my entire worldly wealth, and I only hope that no one will steal it.'

'Sleep in peace, my son,' said the host. 'No harm will come to you in *my* house.'

Early next morning, when the first rays of the sun struck the window sill, the cock saw the millet seed lying there, and promptly gobbled it up. The lad woke up just

as the cock was swallowing it, so he felt very sorry for himself and began to cry; but the farmer, to comfort him, said it was only fair and reasonable that he should take the cock that had eaten his seed.

The lad was delighted at this. He thanked the farmer, took the cock and went on his way. That evening he came to a village, and knocked at a farmhouse door to ask for shelter.

'This cock is my entire worldly wealth,' he said to the farmer before going to bed. 'I only hope that no one will steal it from me.'

'Sleep in peace, my son,' said the farmer. 'No harm will come to you in *my* house.'

Early next morning the cock went out into the farm-yard to look for grain. The farmer's pig found it there and bit its head off. When the lad found his cock lying dead, he felt very sorry for himself and began to cry; but the farmer comforted him, and insisted that he should take the pig that had killed his cock. So he tied a rope to the pig's hind leg, and went on his way.

That evening he came to a village, where a farmer offered him a bed for the night. The lad was glad to accept this hospitality, but said to the farmer, 'This pig is my entire worldly wealth, and I only hope that no one will steal it.'

'Sleep in peace, my son,' said the farmer. 'No harm will come to you in *my* house.'

But next morning a cow caught sight of the strange pig in the courtyard, and tossed it on her horns. When the lad awoke he saw what had happened, and began to cry; but the farmer, to console him, gave him the cow that had tossed his pig.

So the lad tied a rope round the animal's neck and continued on his way. That evening the sun set just as he came to a large mansion, and he asked for shelter for the night. Just as he was going to bed, he went to the lord of the mansion and said, 'This cow is my entire worldly wealth, and I only hope that no one will steal it.'

'Sleep in peace, my son,' said the lord. 'No harm will come to you in *my* house.'

But next morning, when the horses were being watered, one of them, a grey steed, ran wild in the courtyard, and let fly at the strange cow, killing it stone dead. The lad began to cry, but the lord of the mansion felt sorry for him and insisted that he should take the horse that had killed his cow.

So the young fellow mounted his noble horse and rode forth to seek his fortune. At last he came to the Glass Mountain, where he rescued the princess, who was enchanted by an evil spell, and became king of the realm. Just see what a poor lad can do if he is lucky!

The Poor Miller's Boy and the Cat

There was once an old miller who had neither wife nor children, but only three apprentices, who helped with the work in the mill. 'I am no longer young,' he said to them one day, 'and my sole desire is to sit quietly by the fire. Out you go into the world, and I shall gladly hand over the mill to the boy who brings me the finest horse. In return I shall expect him to look after me until my death.'

Now the youngest of the three, whose name was Jack, was considered rather a stupid fellow by the two older boys. All three left the mill together, but when they were a mile or so from the village the older two tried to chase Jack away, saying: 'We don't want you with us, Jack – you'll never find a horse in a million years!'

But Jack followed along behind, and when night fell they turned into a little cave for shelter. The two older ones waited till Jack was asleep, then off they crept and left him lying there.

When daylight came Jack found himself deserted and he was quite scared, for he had not the least idea where he was. He went out of the cave and scrambled over some boulders into the forest, thinking to himself: 'Here I am alone and without a friend in the whole wide world. How on earth can I find a horse?' As he wandered through the trees lost in thought, he met a little spotted cat, who smiled at him.

'Where are you going, Jack?' she asked.

'*You* won't be able to help me!' he replied ungraciously.

'I know very well what it is that you want,' said the cat. 'You are looking for a fine horse! Come and serve me for

seven years, and I will give you the most beautiful horse in the world.'

'What a strange cat!' thought Jack. But he agreed to go with her all the same.

She took him to her enchanted castle, where she had cats to wait on her, running nimbly up and down stairs, having a fine merry time. In the evening at dinner-time three of them made music: one played the double-bass and one the violin, while the third blew the trumpet. When the meal was over, the table was carried away and the tabby cat said, 'Come now, Jack, and dance with me.'

'No,' he replied, 'I have never danced with a cat.'

'Then take him to bed,' she said to the cats.

So one of them showed him to his bedroom, another pulled off his shoes and a third took off his stockings and blew out the candle. Next morning they came again and

helped him to dress: one put on his stockings, another his garters, and the third washed his face and dried it with her tail.

However, Jack too had to serve the tabby cat. Every day he had to chop firewood and he was given a silver axe and a silver saw. So the days went by: he chopped wood, and had all sorts of good things to eat and drink; but he never saw a soul apart from the cat and her servants.

One day she said to him, 'Go out and mow my meadow and spread out the hay to dry.' For this purpose she gave him a silver scythe and a golden whetstone. So off Jack went to the meadow, mowed the hay and spread it out to dry. When he had finished, he took the scythe and whetstone back to the house and asked if he could have his reward.

'No,' said the cat, 'there is something else you must do

for me. I want you to build me a little house. Here are planks and rafters, and a carpenter's axe, and all the materials and tools you will need – all of silver.'

So Jack built the little silver house. When it was ready he said to her that he had done everything she had told him, and he still had no horse, yet the seven years had already passed.

'Would you like to see my horses, Jack?' asked the cat.

'Yes, please!' said Jack.

She opened the doors of the little silver house, and there stood twelve silver horses, gleaming and glittering, the most beautiful horses he had ever seen.

'Go home now,' she said, and she gave him food and drink to take with him. 'I cannot give you your horse yet, but I will follow with it in three days' time.'

She pointed out the way to the mill, and Jack set out. But all the time he had been with her, she had not given him any new clothes, and he was still wearing the worn and patched old things which he had brought with him seven years previously, and which were now far too small for him.

When he reached the mill he found that the other two boys had arrived before him, with their horses; but one horse was blind, and the other lame.

'Where is your horse, Jack?' they asked.

'It will be following in three days' time.'

'Indeed,' they laughed. 'It must be a fine horse that can come on its own!'

Jack went into the parlour, but the miller was shocked to see him in such rags and tatters, and would not allow him to sit down at table, so they gave him a bowl of food to eat outside in the yard. When the two older boys went to bed at night they would not give Jack a bed, and he had to creep into the goose-hut and lie down on the straw.

On the morning after the three days had gone by, there rolled up to the mill a coach drawn by six silver horses, gleaming and glittering, with a serving man following behind with a seventh horse, which was for the poor miller's boy. The door of the coach opened and out stepped a beautiful princess, and this princess was the spotted cat whom Jack had served for seven years. She went into the mill and asked for him.

'We could not have him in the mill,' said the miller. 'He was so tattered and torn that we had to put him in the goose-hut.'

The princess told them to fetch him, so they went and brought him to her. A footman laid out magnificent clothes for him, and he had to wash and change; and when he was ready no king could have looked more smart and handsome. The princess called her serving-man to bring the seventh horse before the miller, saying, 'This is for the miller's third apprentice.'

'Then he must have the mill,' exclaimed the miller.

But the princess laughed, and said, 'Keep your mill!' She took Jack by the hand and led him to her coach, and they drove away.

They drove to the little silver house which he had built for her with the silver tools. But it had turned into a great castle, in which everything was made of silver. So they were married, and he was so rich that he had more than enough for the rest of his life, and they lived very happily together.

The Old Wizard and the Children

There was once a wicked old wizard who had kidnapped a little boy and girl, and he lived with them in a damp and dingy cave. He possessed a book of magic, from which he had learnt all his magic spells. This book was his most treasured possession, and he looked after it with particular care.

In time the little boy found out where the book was hidden, so whenever the horrid old wizard went out of the cave and left the children on their own, the boy would bring out the book and read it, with the result that he acquired a great deal of magic lore.

One day the wizard left the cave bright and early, so the boy shook his little sister awake and whispered, 'Now's our chance! Get ready this instant, and we shall be far away from here before he returns!' So off they went, and ran over hill and dale all day long.

Towards evening the wizard returned to his cave and found the children gone. He opened his book of magic, and saw immediately which direction they had taken, and he hurried after them. Before long he had almost overtaken them.

But the children heard the old man shouting behind them, and the little girl cried, 'Now we are lost, brother! The wicked wizard is close behind us!'

Then the boy quickly pronounced a magic spell, which he had learnt from the book, and turned himself into a pond and his little sister into a fish swimming about in it.

The old wizard saw how he had been cheated, and roared in a fury, 'Just you wait, I'll soon catch you!'

So he ran quickly back to the cave and fetched a fishing net, so that he could catch the little fish. But as soon as he had gone the fish was again a little girl and the pond a little boy, and off they ran as fast as their legs would carry them.

Before long the wicked wizard arrived at the spot where the pond had been, but he saw only a beautiful meadow covered with lovely flowers; there was no sign of either pond or fish. This infuriated him more than ever. He threw the net away and raised his magic wand, which pointed in the direction the children had taken.

By the time he caught up with them it was growing dark. They heard him bellowing when he was some distance off, and once again the little girl cried, 'Now we are lost, brother! The wicked wizard is close behind us!'

So again the little boy pronounced a magic spell, which he had learnt from the book, and in the twinkling of an eye he turned into a wayside chapel, while his little sister was a beautiful statue above the altar.

When the wizard saw the chapel he was furious, but he dared not go inside, for a chapel is holy ground and forbidden to wicked wizards. Then in his rage he shouted, 'If I cannot come in, I can at least burn you to ashes!' And off he rushed to the cave to fetch fire, with his long red cloak streaming behind him.

Quick as lightning the chapel and statue were once again a little boy and girl, and off they ran.

Not long afterwards the wizard returned with a lighted faggot to the place where the chapel had been, but he found only an enormous boulder, and he could hardly set fire to that. Foaming with rage he followed the children's trail.

After a little while he caught sight of them again, and the little girl spied him over her shoulder.

'Now we are lost indeed, brother!' she cried. 'The wicked wizard is close behind us!'

For the third time the little boy pronounced a magic spell, and he was changed on the spot into a barn, while his sister was a little ear of corn on the floor.

As soon as the wizard saw what had happened, he turned himself into a black cock to gobble up the corn. As fast as he could the little boy uttered another magic spell, and turned himself into a fox. Before the black cock could reach the corn, the fox sprang on him and bit his head off.

And so that was the well-deserved end of the wicked wizard.

The Three Feathers

There was once a king who had three sons; the two eldest were unkind to the youngest, and called him Simpleton.

The king was unable to decide which of his three sons should inherit the realm and become king after him. So he thought for a while, and said, 'Go out into the world, and whoever brings me the finest carpet shall be king when I am dead.' And he took them outside the castle and blew three feathers into the air, saying, 'You must go wherever they lead you. And you must be back before the moon is full.'

Now one feather flew to the east, another to the west, but the third one flew straight up in the air and finally came to rest on the ground a few yards away. So the two older brothers went east and west, but Simpleton had to stay where his feather landed.

Simpleton sat down and was sad at heart, until he noticed a little trap-door just where the feather lay on the ground. He lifted it up, and saw a staircase descending into the darkness below. Down he went, until he came to another door, on which he knocked. From inside came a deep voice calling:

> 'Little green maiden,
> Go, hop and see
> Who knocks at our door.
> Who can it be?'

The door opened, and he saw an enormous fat toad sitting on the floor, surrounded by smaller toads. She asked what he wanted, and he replied, 'I should like the most beautiful carpet in the world.' Then she called a young toad, saying:

> 'Little green maiden,
> Go, hop away
> And bring the great box
> As quick as you may.'

So the young toad brought a great box of gold and silver and laid it before her. She opened it and drew out a carpet so beautiful that it could not have been woven on this earth. Simpleton thanked her and climbed into the world.

Meanwhile the two older brothers had taken little trouble to find a fine carpet, for they had spent their time in feasting and making merry; so just before the moon was full they took some coarse sackcloth from the first shepherds' wives they met, and rode back with it hastily to the king.

They arrived back at the same time as Simpleton, who was carrying his beautiful carpet, and when the king saw it he was filled with amazement. 'There is no doubt,' he said, 'that the crown should go to Simpleton.'

But the two older brothers let their father have no peace. 'You cannot possibly be serious!' they exclaimed. 'How *can* Simpleton be king, when he is so stupid?' And they persuaded him to make a new arrangement.

So the king announced that the kingdom would be given to the one who brought him the most beautiful ring; and once again he took his three sons outside the castle, and blew three feathers into the air. 'Go where they lead you,' he said, 'and be back before the moon is full.'

Once again the two older sons went to the east and to

the west, and Simpleton's feather floated down only a few yards away beside the trap-door. Down he went again, and told the fat toad that he needed the most beautiful ring in the world. She sent for her great silver and gold box and gave him a golden ring covered with jewels, which was much more beautiful than any that a goldsmith on this earth could have made.

Now the two older brothers again wasted their days in feasting and making merry, and they left no time to search properly for a ring. At the last moment the first brother begged an old curtain ring from the first house he came to on his homeward journey. The second brother met a farmer ploughing his field and for a few pence he bought one of the rings from the horse's harness. These two rings they took back to the king. But when Simpleton pulled out his beautiful golden ring covered with jewels, the king's eyes sparkled. 'The crown must indeed go to Simpleton,' he said. 'There is not the slightest doubt.'

The two older brothers pestered the king, however, until he agreed to make a third condition. 'Whoever brings home the most beautiful woman,' he said, 'shall inherit the kingdom.' Once again he blew the feathers into the air, and they flew east, west and straight upwards. 'Go where they lead you,' he said, 'and be back before the moon is full.'

Once again Simpleton descended to the fat toad, and told her he must take home the most beautiful woman in the world.

'That is not so easy!' she replied. 'But we will see what we can do for you.' And she gave him a turnip. The turnip had been hollowed out, and six white mice had been harnessed to it.

'What am I to do with this?' asked Simpleton in consternation.

'Put one of my little toads inside,' replied the fat toad. So he selected a little toad at random from the circle round about, and laid her inside the turnip. She immediately turned into the most beautiful girl he had ever set eyes on; the turnip became a coach, and the six white mice became six white horses. So he kissed the girl and drove off quickly with her to the king.

His brothers again had left no time to do their seeking, but they had brought along the first peasant women they had happened to meet. When the king saw them he no longer had any doubts, but declared that the crown would go to Simpleton.

Once again, however, the other two brothers made a frightful fuss. They insisted that the women should leap through a great iron ring which hung from the ceiling, for they thought that the peasant women were strong and

agile, but that the slender girl whom Simpleton had brought would jump to her death.

The king agreed, and the two peasant women jumped

through the ring, but so clumsily that they fell heavily to the floor, and one broke her legs and the other her arms. Then the beautiful girl leapt through the ring as lightly as a deer, and put an end to all opposition. So Simpleton was given the crown, and has ruled wisely ever since.

Nut-cracker

Two boys were gathering hazel nuts in the woods, and they sat down under a tree in order to eat what they had gathered. But neither of them had a knife with him, and they could not bite the nuts open with their teeth.

'What a shame!' they cried. 'If only someone would come along who could open these nuts for us!'

Hardly had they said this when a strange little man came walking through the woods. Such an odd-looking fellow they had never seen before. He had a big, big head, from which a long stiff plait hung down to his heels behind him, and he wore a little golden hat, a red gown and yellow boots. As he trotted towards them he sang this song:

> 'Crick! Crack! Crick! Crack!
> Cracking through the woods I go
> Where the nuts are hanging low,
> Where I see before my eyes
> Nuts of every shape and size,
> Nuts for breaking, nuts for crunching,
> Nuts for biting, nuts for munching,
> Crick! Crack! Crick! Crack!
> Cracking through the woods I go!'

The two boys could hardly help bursting into laughter

at the strange little creature, whom they took to be a woodland dwarf. 'If you want nuts to crack,' they called to him, 'come and crack these for us, so that we can eat them.'

The little man began to sing again:

> 'Here I see you've nuts in plenty;
> If I bite and crack you twenty,
> Will you give me for my trouble
> Some of them for me to nibble?'

'Yes,' cried the boys. 'You can share them with us!' The little man stepped up to them and sang:

> 'Crick! Crack! Crick! Crack!
> Lift up the plait behind my back.
> Crack! Crick! Crack! Crick!
> Between my teeth the nuts must stick.
> Crick! Crack! Crick! Crack!
> Pull down the plait behind my back,
> Crack! Crick! Crack! Crick!
> And that, you'll find, will do the trick.'

They did just as he told them, and they laughed each time they took hold of the little man by his long stiff plait, heard the sharp crick! crack! and saw the nut spring out of his mouth.

Soon all the nuts were cracked and the little man sang:

> 'Crick! Crack! Crick! Crack!
> Let me have some of them back!'

One of the boys was quite ready to give the little man the promised reward, but the other boy was mean and wicked and prevented him, saying, 'Why give our nuts to that fellow? We want them for ourselves! Off you go, Nutcracker, and gather your own nuts!'

The nutcracker grew angry, and sang:

> 'Did we not agree,
> That some were for me?
> If you eat them instead,
> I'll bite off your head!'

The wicked boy laughed at this. 'Bite off my head?' he said. 'You had better be going, or I'll give you a crack with my stick!' And he threatened the nutcracker with the stick he had been using to knock the hazel nuts down. The nutcracker turned purple with rage. He reached behind him and lifted up his own long stiff plait – crick! crack! The nutcracker's teeth snapped together, and the wicked boy's head was gone.

That is the story of the first nutcracker. His children and his grandchildren will do the same to your fingers, if you don't take care.

The Fox and the Hedgehog

A fox was tremendously hungry. He ran to and fro all over a newly ploughed field, looking for mice, till suddenly he stumbled over a hedgehog who was sitting with a dead mouse in her paws.

'Thief!' cried the fox angrily. 'What right has a prickly pig like you to such a tasty morsel?' And he snatched the mouse from under the hedgehog's nose, and swallowed it.

'May you choke on it, you thieving wretch!' spluttered the hedgehog.

But the fox only laughed at the hedgehog's anger. 'Tell me,' he asked, 'why do you look like a sort of pin-cushion?'

'These prickles are my only defence,' replied the hedge-hog.

'You poor thing!' said the fox with a sneer. 'Thank God I have no need for any weapons of that sort – my cunning pulls me through all my difficulties!'

Suddenly they heard a commotion – Halloo! Halloo! – as two greyhounds broke through the undergrowth and came streaking across the field. Quick as thought the hedgehog curled herself into a ball, while the fox took to his heels and ran. The dogs snuffled a bit at the hedgehog, but had their noses pricked for their pains, so they left it alone and rushed off after the fox.

Now the fox tried all the cunning he knew. He darted to and fro in a zig-zag, doubled back round behind the haystacks and played a hundred and one tricks – but all in vain. The dogs caught him and seized him by the ears, and dragged him before their master, the huntsman.

The Fox and the Snail

A fox was feeling rather pleased with himself, and ran round the meadow, prancing and leaping. He spotted a snail sliding through the grass, and began to laugh at it and make fun of the little creature.

'Hullo, you tiny thing!' he said. 'I've never seen a snail moving before! How would you like to try a race with me?'

The snail stretched out his four horns, looked right and left, and inspected the fox with all four eyes. 'Why not?' he replied. 'I accept your challenge with very great pleasure!'

So they agreed to race to the bank of the stream, which was about a hundred yards away.

'I'll give you a start of the length of your whole body,' said the snail, 'and I bet I'll be there before you!'

The fox simply could not understand this at all. How *could* such a tiny creature run faster than he could?

Now the snail clung to the tip of the fox's tail, and cried, 'Are you ready? I'll give the word to go.' So he counted, 'One, two, three, go!' Off flew the fox as fast as the wind, and soon reached the bank of the stream. He swung round to see if the snail was coming, and flicked the little creature from the tip of his tail over to the other side of the stream.

'Where are you, slowcoach!' he shouted.

'I have been here for ages!' replied the snail from the far bank. 'I was tired waiting for you, so I just swam across the stream.'

The fox was so ashamed that he tucked his tail between his legs and slunk away without saying a word.

The Wolf and the Fox

A wolf had a fox with him, and made him do all his dirty work. The fox would gladly have escaped, but the wolf was stronger than he was, so he had to do as he was told.

One day, as they went through the forest, the wolf said, 'Off you go, Red Fox, and bring me something good to eat, or I'll eat you instead!'

'I know a farm,' replied the fox, 'where there are a number of little lambs. I'll bring you one if you like.'

This suited the wolf very well, so the fox went and stole a lamb and brought it back to the wolf, who devoured it. But the wolf was still hungry, and thought he would go and steal another lamb for himself. Off he went to the farm, but he was so clumsy about it that the ewe saw him and started to bleat, and she made such a noise that the farm people came running up with all sorts of farm implements. They beat the wolf so mercilessly that he fled, limping and groaning.

'You've made a fool of me,' complained the wolf when he reached the fox. 'When I tried to steal another lamb, all the farm people rushed out, and they have beaten me to a jelly!'

'Why must you be so greedy?' replied the fox.

Next day they were strolling through the forest, when the wolf said, 'Bring me something to eat, Red Fox, or I'll eat you instead!'

'I know a farm,' replied the fox, 'where the farmer's wife bakes wonderful pancakes. I'll bring some if you like.'

Off he went, and when he came to the farm-house he sniffed around for a time till he discovered the dish of pancakes, took out six and carried them back to the wolf. 'There you are!' he said, and went off to sleep.

The wolf swallowed all six pancakes at one gulp, and wanted more. So off he went to the farm-house, and clumsily pulled the whole dish off the shelf, so that it was broken into pieces on the floor. The farmer's wife came to

see what all the noise was, and when she saw the wolf she raised the alarm. Up rushed all the farm people, who beat him with sticks and rakes and pitchforks until he was lame in two legs, and he fled howling into the forest.

'You've made a fool of me,' he complained to the fox. 'The farm people caught me and almost beat the life out of me!'

'Why must you be so greedy?' replied the fox.

Again on the third day they were going through the forest, the wolf limping along with difficulty. 'Red Fox,' he said, 'go and bring something to eat, or I'll eat you instead!'

'I know a man,' replied the fox, 'who has a great barrel of salted meat lying in his cellar. Let's go and eat it.'

'Fine,' said the wolf. 'But I want you to help me if we are attacked.'

'All right,' replied the fox, and showed him the way to the cellar.

There was plenty of meat in the barrel, and the wolf

tucked in and made a hearty meal of it. The fox ate a little too, but he kept running back to the hole by which they had entered, to see if his body was still slim enough to slip through it.

'Tell me, dear fox,' said the wolf, 'why are you so restless?'

'I just want to make sure that no one is coming,' replied the crafty animal. 'Don't eat too much!'

'I shall go on eating till the barrel is empty!' declared the wolf.

Meanwhile, the owner of the house had been disturbed by all the noise, and came to see what was happening. As soon as the fox caught sight of him, he was out in a flash; but the wolf had eaten so much that he stuck in the hole, and could move neither forwards nor backwards.

The man seized a cudgel and struck the wolf dead, and the fox trotted off through the trees, delighted to be rid of the old glutton.

The Clever Blue Tit and the Fox

A fox had found nothing to eat, and came ravenous with hunger to a tree where a blue tit had her nest.

'Give me your little ones!' he called up to the mother tit, 'or I'll knock the tree down and eat you *all* up.'

The poor blue tit was terrified, and could not think what to do. 'Dear fox,' she said at last, 'leave my little ones alone. They are so very tiny, that they would hardly give you a mouthful. If you would like to find food in plenty, follow me.'

'All right, let's see!' replied the fox.

So the blue tit flew off, while the fox followed some distance behind, till they found two women sitting gossiping by the roadside, with their baskets of bread and cakes lying on the grass beside them. While the fox lay concealed in the bushes, the blue tit began to hop and flutter about as if her wing were broken. The women jumped up and tried to catch the little bird, but she fluttered further and further away.

Out crept the fox and gobbled up everything that was in the baskets, and when the blue tit saw this she took to the air and flew back to her nest, leaving the two women to wonder what had happened to their bread and cakes.

The fox, however, returned to the blue tit's tree and looked up at the nest. 'Oho!' he said, 'you have not done enough for me yet. Go and find me something to drink!'

'All right,' replied the tit. 'Follow me!' And she flew back to the road, where they found a man carrying a barrel of wine on his cart. The little tit perched on the end of the barrel, and began to peck at it. The man took one or two swipes at her with his whip, but she flitted to and fro, avoiding the blows, and went on pecking. This infuriated the man, who seized his axe and aimed a blow at her; but she hopped out of the way just in time, so that the axe sank deep into the barrel and let the wine pour all over the road. Then the fox crept out of the bushes, and drank the wine.

'Does that satisfy you?' asked the blue tit.

'Not yet,' declared the fox. 'I want you to make me laugh!'

'All right, follow me,' cried the tit as she flew off. She led him to a barn, where there were two men hard at work

threshing the corn – a young man, and an older man with a bald head. The fox clambered up to the hay-loft to watch the fun, while the blue tit settled on the old man's bald head. He tried to sweep her off with his hand, but she fluttered up for an instant, and came back again as soon as he took his hand away.

This exasperated the man, who called to the younger thresher, 'Knock it off, Stephen!' So Stephen took a swipe at the tit with his threshing flail, but the tit hopped off just in time, so that the old man was struck on his bald head and knocked to the ground.

134

This made the fox laugh so heartily that he fell off the hayloft and hurtled to the floor below. Both men set about the fox so violently with their threshing flails that the hide was almost beaten off him, and he was lucky to be able to creep out of the barn, more dead than alive.

Pleased with her day's work, the little blue tit flew back to her nest.

The Wee Folk

There was once a cobbler who was so poor, through no fault of his own, that he had only enough leather left for a single pair of shoes. He cut the leather all ready into shape one evening, meaning to sew it into shoes the following morning. Because he was a good man, he said his prayers, and then he went to bed.

Next morning when he came down to work, he found the shoes lying ready on the table. He could not understand it at all, for he knew that *he* had not sewn them. He picked them up to have a closer look at them, and found them so well made that there was not a single stitch wrong, so that they looked a perfect masterpiece.

It was not long before a customer called at the shop, and he was so pleased with the shoes that he paid more than the usual price, and this enabled the cobbler to buy enough for two more pairs. Once again he cut the leather before going to bed, and next morning he rose early to finish the work. But there was no need to, for the shoes were ready on the table when he got up.

He soon sold these to customers who gave him enough

money to buy leather for four more pairs of shoes, and early next morning he found four pairs lying ready on the table. And so it went on: whatever leather he cut in the evening was made up into shoes by the following morning, so that before long he began to grow quite rich.

Now one evening shortly before Christmas the man had an idea. 'Let's stay up,' he whispered to his wife before going to bed, 'and see who it is who is helping us.' His wife agreed, and they hid themselves behind some clothes in the corner, and waited without making a sound.

On the stroke of midnight two funny little men as naked as could be, came and sat down at the cobbler's table. There they began to stitch and sew and hammer so quickly and so skilfully that the cobbler's eyes almost popped out of his head. Before long the work was finished and the little men ran off, leaving the shoes on the table.

Next morning the cobbler's wife had an idea. 'These little men have made us rich,' she said to her husband, 'and we ought to show our gratitude. They must be frozen running around like that without any clothes. I should like to make them little shirts, coats, waistcoats and trousers, and knit them each a pair of stockings; you can make them each a little pair of boots.'

The cobbler thought this was an excellent idea, so that evening they laid their presents on the table instead of the leather, and hid in the corner to see what would happen.

On the stroke of midnight the two little naked men came running in, ready to set to work; they seemed surprised to find no leather, but when they saw two sets of clothes, neatly folded at either end of the table, they were delighted. They quickly dressed themselves and then they danced on the table, singing:

'Now we are clad for any weather,
Why should we bother sewing leather?'

They hopped and skipped and leapt over chairs and benches, until at last they danced out of the door. They never came back, but the cobbler's affairs prospered as long as he lived.

The Fox and the Stork

A fox and a stork had struck up a friendship, and one fine day the fox asked the stork to supper. 'Do come, my dear friend,' she said. 'I want you to try my special broth.'

The stork came to the feast, and found that the fox had poured out an enormous plateful of the special broth. She placed it before the stork saying, 'Come and eat, my dear friend. I made the broth myself.'

In his efforts to eat the broth the stork tapped and clattered his beak against the plate, even thrusting it sideways into the broth, but not a single drop could he suck up. Meanwhile the fox had quickly lapped up the whole plateful, and she licked the plate clean, saying, 'I'm afraid that's all there is, dear stork. I hope you have enjoyed it!'

'Thank you very much, my dear friend,' replied the stork. 'Tomorrow you must come and have supper with me.'

So next evening the fox went to the stork's house for supper. The stork had prepared a most wonderful fish soup. He poured it into a jug with a long narrow neck, and put the jug between them, saying, 'There you are, my dear friend. I'm sure you will like it.'

The fox walked round and round the jug, examining it from all angles, sniffing the delicious aroma and licking the rim of the jug, but not a drop did she taste, for she could not reach the soup through the long narrow neck. The stork, on the other hand, sipped and sucked the soup up with his long beak until it was all finished.

'I'm afraid that is all, my dear friend!' he said to the fox. 'Wasn't it good?'

From that day to this there has never been any great friendship between storks and foxes.

The Water-sprite

A little boy and girl were playing beside a well, when they both slipped, and in they fell together. Down in the well dwelt a water-sprite, who grabbed them, saying, 'Now you must stay and work for me!'

She gave the little girl some horrid tangled flax to spin, and made her fetch water in a bucket which had holes in it. The little boy had to cut down a great oak tree with a blunt axe, and they were given nothing to eat but stale bread as hard as stone.

Before long the children were so tired of this treatment that one Sunday, while the water-sprite was at church, they ran away. When church was over, the water-sprite saw that the children had gone, so she followed them with great leaps and bounds. They saw her coming from some way off, so the little girl threw a brush over her shoulder. It sprang up into an enormous hill with thousands of spikes, over which the water-sprite had to clamber as well as she could.

At last she struggled over, and when the children saw her catching them up once more the little boy threw a comb over his shoulder. It sprang up into an immense ridge with thousands of pinnacles upon it.

The water-sprite began to scramble up it, with great difficulty, for she was almost caught among the pinnacles, but at last she was over. The little girl then threw a mirror over her shoulder. This grew into a glass mountain, which was so smooth that the water-sprite could not possibly climb it.

She thought to herself, 'I will go home and fetch my magic axe and cleave the glass mountain in two.' However, long before she came back the children were safe, and the water-sprite had to return to her well.

The Sun-child

There was once a woman who had no children, and this caused her great sorrow.

'Dear Sun,' she said one warm summer's day, 'give me

a baby girl, and I will give her back to you when she is twelve years old.' So the sun gave her a little girl, who was called Letiko, and the woman was extremely fond of her.

Now when Letiko was twelve years old, she went one day to gather wild flowers in the meadow, and the sun came to her, saying, 'Letiko, go and tell your mother that the time has come for her to keep her promise to me.'

So Letiko went home, and told her mother that a fine gentleman had told her that it was time for her mother's promise to be kept. Her mother turned pale with fright, and rushed to close all the doors and windows in the house, to prevent the sun from coming in. She blocked up every crack and chink through which the sun might have entered.

But she forgot the keyhole, and through this the sun sent a sunbeam, which seized Letiko and took her off to the sun.

Now one day the sun sent Letiko into the barn to fetch some straw. She sat down on one of the bales and began to cry.

'Just as you sigh beneath me, straw,' she said, 'so my heart sighs for my dear mother.'

She was so long away that when she came back the sun asked her, 'What is the matter, Letiko? Why were you away for so long?'

'My slippers are so big,' she replied, 'that I can hardly walk in them.'

So the sun made her slippers a little smaller.

On another occasion the sun sent her to the spring for water, and she sat down beside the spring and cried.

'Just as you flow past me, water, so flows my heart with longing to my dear mother.'

Again she was a long time away, so when she came back the sun asked her, 'What is the matter, Letiko? Why were you away for so long?'

'My dress is too long, and I trip over it when I walk,' she said.

So the sun cut her dress a little shorter.

Not long afterwards he sent her for a pair of sandals. As Letiko was carrying them back she again began to cry.

'Just as you creak, leather, so my heart creaks for my dear mother.'

'What is the matter, Letiko?' asked the sun once again. 'Why were you away for so long?'

'My hat is too wide and it fell over my eyes,' she replied.

So the sun made her hat a little narrower.

But the sun was well aware of Letiko's sadness, for he had heard her crying for her mother. So he sent for two young hares, and asked them if they would be willing to take Letiko back to her.

'Yes, indeed,' they replied.

'What will you eat and drink,' asked the sun, 'if you are hungry and thirsty on the way?'

'We shall eat grass, and drink the sparkling waters of the streams,' they replied.

'All right,' said the sun. 'Look after her carefully and take her home to her mother.'

So the two young hares set off with Letiko, but it was a long, long way to her mother's house, and the hares began to feel hungry.

'Dear Letiko,' they said, 'climb this tree and stay there in safety until we have eaten.'

So the hares went off to look for fresh green grass, while Letiko sat in the fork of the tree and looked round about her. Suddenly a wicked witch appeared below, and said,

'Come down, my child, come and see what beautiful shoes I have!'

'Oh, my shoes are much more beautiful than yours!' replied Letiko.

'Quickly, my child, hurry up!' said the witch. 'It is time I was sweeping out my house!'

'Go and sweep it then,' said Letiko, 'and come back here when you've finished.'

So the witch went away and swept out her house, and returned beneath the tree, calling up, 'Come down, my child, come and see what lovely clothes I have!'

'Oh, my clothes are much more lovely than yours!' replied Letiko.

'Come down at once, do you hear!' cried the witch, stamping her foot with rage. 'If you don't come, I will chop the tree down and eat you up!'

'Very well,' said Letiko. 'Chop it down and eat me up!'

So the witch hacked away, but she could not chop down the tree.

''Letiko, Letiko,' she called up once more, 'my children are hungry and want their food.'

'Then go and feed them, and come back here when you have finished.'

Off went the witch, and without wasting an instant Letiko called, 'Little hares, little hares, come here!' The two hares came bounding back to the tree, so Letiko climbed down and off they went as fast as possible.

But the witch followed after them and tried to catch them.

Her way lay across a field where she saw people working.

'Did anyone pass this way?' she asked.

The people replied, 'We are planting beans.'

'Beans?' exclaimed the witch. 'I asked you if anyone had passed this way.'

'Can you not hear?' said the people. 'We are planting beans, beans, *beans*!'

The witch scowled at them and hurried on her way.

Meanwhile Letiko was near home.

The cat, who was sitting in the sunshine on the roof, blinked her eyes and cried, 'Miaow! Miaow! Letiko is coming!'

'You miserable cat,' said Letiko's mother, 'do you want to break my heart?'

Then the dog saw her coming, pricked up his ears and barked, 'Woof! Woof! Letiko is coming!'

'You miserable dog,' said Letiko's mother, 'do you want to break my heart?'

The cock, who was perched on the gate, shook his red comb and crowed, 'Cock-a-doodle-doo! Letiko is coming.'

'You miserable bird,' said Letiko's mother, 'do you want to break my heart?'

At that very moment Letiko and the two hares slipped

through the gate and in at the door. The witch was close behind, and she grabbed one of the hares by the tail and pulled the tail right off. Then she vanished.

Letiko's mother flung both arms round her neck and wept for joy. Then she turned to the hare who had lost his tail, saying, 'Dear hare, you have brought me back my Letiko, so I will make you a beautiful new tail of silver.'

This she did, and from that day onwards Letiko and her mother lived happily together. The two hares settled down near the cottage and brought up a family of six beautiful baby hares, and three of them had silver tails, just like their father's.

The Birch Twig

There once was a mother who was so poor that all she could afford to cook for herself and her son to eat was a thin watery soup. One day she found she had no firewood left in the house, so she said to her son, 'Go out into the forest and gather wood, for I haven't a single twig left to warm the soup. But tomorrow is Sunday, so be sure to bring plenty.'

The boy wasted no time, but went into a thick part of the forest where he worked so hard collecting wood that the sweat poured down his brow. With great difficulty he loaded the enormous bundle on to his back, and set off for home.

As he was staggering through the trees, tired and hungry, he saw a little old woman in front of him, whose face was wrinkled like a walnut. At her feet lay a bundle of firewood, and she complained that she was old and tired and could carry it no further. 'Please will you help me?' she asked him.

'I'm afraid my own bundle is all I can manage,' replied the boy, 'and I cannot keep my mother waiting any longer.'

'But you are young and strong,' said the old woman. 'You can carry the wood for me to my little hut, and still be home in good time. It is not far from here, and I will pay you well.'

'A fine payment that will be,' thought the boy, 'for she herself has nothing.' Nevertheless he felt sorry for her because she was so old and weak, so he laid his own bundle down, lifted up her bundle of twigs, and followed her through the forest.

Before long they had reached her little hut. 'Wait here,' she said as he dumped the wood on the ground. 'I must fetch your wages.'

The boy was curious to see what she would bring him, but he did not have long to wait before she came back holding a birch twig in her hand. She seemed to have grown taller, and she appeared so solemn and so awe-inspiring that he felt almost afraid of her.

'You are a good lad,' she said, 'willing to help poor old

folk like me, and this is your reward. Take this birch twig and keep it carefully, for it will bear you golden fruit.' She handed him the twig and disappeared into the hut.

The boy nearly burst out laughing at this strange present, but he kept it and ran back to his own bundle of wood, loaded it on to his back and plodded homewards. By this time he was so exhausted with his hard work that his eyes kept closing, and he thought he would have a rest. He laid his bundle down, stuck his birch twig into the ground and fell asleep.

Not until evening did he wake up, when the sun was sinking low through the trees and the cool night breeze was already stirring the leaves overhead. He rubbed the sleep from his eyes and looked at the bundle of firewood and his birch twig. To his amazement he found that the twig had grown into a beautiful little tree, with shining golden leaves and fruit. Full of excitement he sprang up and began to pluck them, stuffing them into his haversack. When it was full to the very top, he fastened it tightly and raced home as fast as his legs would carry him, leaving the bundle of wood lying.

His mother had been waiting for him for a long time, and was worried in case he had met with an accident. When she saw him coming without wood, but beaming all over his face, she was very angry. 'Where have you been all day?' she scolded him. 'I sent you into the forest early this morning to fetch firewood. Now it is almost dark, and yet you bring me none!'

'Don't be angry, Mother,' said the boy. 'I have been working extremely hard, and I am sure you will be pleased with me.' So saying he shook the golden leaves and fruit on to the table, where they sparkled and glittered. His mother's eyes almost popped out of her head. She could not help feeling, however, that all these riches could not have been earned honestly, so she asked him where they had come from. She was delighted when she heard the whole story, and from that day to this neither mother nor son has lacked anything that this world's riches can buy.

The Devil and the Seamstress

A long, long time ago there lived a woman who was so quick and so skilful with her needle that it would have been hard to find her equal. But she was conceited, and one day – half in jest and half in earnest – she rashly said that she would challenge the devil himself to a sewing contest.

But the devil hears a great deal more than we think, and our words and even our whispers carry right down to the depths of hell. So he heard what the woman said, and came to take her at her word. At first she was terrified and denied uttering the challenge, but the devil insisted, so they agreed to compete to see who could make a shirt first. If the woman lost the competition, however, the devil was to take her down with him to hell.

The contest began with the cutting out, but neither of them had the advantage, for they both took exactly the same time. When it came to sewing, however, you would have been amazed at the devil's ignorance! In order to avoid wasting time re-threading his needle later, he threaded a whole bobbin of cotton at once and that was not very clever, for at each stitch he had to run three times round the house in order to pull the thread through. And as he had forgotten to tie a knot in the end, he ran the first three times round in vain!

The seamstress threaded her needle just as she always did, and remembered to tie a strong knot in the end, just as

she always did. Then she sewed and sewed, without looking up, until the shirt was finished. And when it was ready she threw it at the devil as he came puffing round the house, with a face as black as thunder. He was so ashamed that he sank into the ground in a glow of flames, for he had not finished a single seam.

That is how the devil lost his contest, and from that day to this he has never accepted another sewing challenge. You may still hear people say, when anyone has done a thoroughly clumsy job of work, 'He is just like the devil, who had to run three times round the house for every stitch.'

The Seven Ravens

A man had seven sons but no daughters, although he had always longed for one. When at long last a daughter was born, he was delighted.

The baby was very frail and it was necessary to baptize her at once. The man sent his sons to the well to fetch water for the baptism, but they quarrelled over the jug, for each of them wanted to carry it back for his baby sister, and the jug fell into the well and was lost. There they all stood, feeling ashamed of themselves, none daring to go and tell their father.

After a time, when there was no sign of them, their father became impatient. 'I am sure they have gone off to play and forgotten all about the baptism!' he said. He was very angry, for he was afraid that the baby would die un-

baptized, and in his anger he cried, 'May they all be turned
into ravens!'

Immediately there was a whirring of wings overhead,
and, looking up, he saw seven pitch-black ravens flying
away.

Neither mother nor father could take back the curse.
They were heartbroken over the loss of their seven sons,
but comforted themselves a little with their pretty little

daughter, who gained strength every day. She grew into a beautiful little girl, loved by every one who saw her. For a long time she had no idea that she had any brothers, until one day she overheard some people talking about her. 'She is indeed a beautiful girl,' they said, 'but she is the cause of her brothers' misfortune.'

She was worried when she heard this, and went to her father and mother. 'Is it true that I have brothers?' she asked. 'Where have they gone?' The time had come when her parents could keep their secret no longer, but they told her that she was in no way to blame for her brothers' misfortune, which was sent by heaven.

But the girl had no peace of mind until she left home secretly, and went out into the wide world to search for her brothers. She took with her a ring belonging to her mother for a keepsake, a loaf of bread for when she was hungry, and a jug of water for when she was thirsty.

On she wandered, far, far into the wide world, until she came to the place where the sun dwelt, but that was far too hot. She hurried away to where the moon dwelt, but that was far too cold and frightening, and as soon as the moon caught sight of her it said, 'Oho! I smell the flesh of a little girl!'

Away she ran, and came to where the stars dwelt, each one sitting on its little chair. They were sympathetic towards her, and the Morning Star rose and handed her a magic bone, saying, 'Without that bone you will not be able to open the Glass Mountain, and that is where you will find your brothers.'

She thanked the Morning Star and took the bone, which she wrapped in a handkerchief, and away she went until she came to the Glass Mountain. The door was locked, and

she looked for the magic bone in her handkerchief. But the handkerchief was empty and she had lost the gift that the stars had made her. What was she to do? The little sister took a knife, cut off her own little finger, fitted it into the lock and opened the door.

She went through and the door clicked shut behind her, and she found herself face to face with a little dwarf. 'What do you seek, my child?' asked the dwarf.

'I seek my brothers,' she replied, 'the seven ravens.'

'The ravens are not at home,' said the dwarf, 'but come in and wait till they return.'

While she was waiting, the dwarf carried in the ravens' supper on seven little plates and in seven little tumblers. From each plate she ate a morsel, and from each tumbler she took a sip, and when she had come to the last tumbler she dropped her mother's ring into it.

Suddenly she heard the whirring of wings. 'Here are the ravens flying home,' said the dwarf. In they flew, and settled beside their supper. 'Who has been eating from my plate?' asked one. 'And who has been drinking from my tumbler?' asked another. 'This is the mark of human lips!'

When the seventh raven came to the bottom of his tumbler he found the ring and he knew it belonged to his mother. 'God grant that our sister be here,' he declared, 'for then we shall be set free from this enchantment!'

The girl, who had been hiding behind the door all this time, stepped forth when she heard these words, and all the ravens were restored to their human shape. There was great merry-making and rejoicing that evening, and next morning they all went happily home together.

The Snow-wife

A widow had two daughters, of whom one was beautiful and hard-working, the other ugly and lazy. The widow was fonder of the ugly, lazy girl, because she was her own daughter. The other was her stepdaughter, and she was made to do all the work about the house. What time there was left she had to spend sitting by the well and spinning wool until her fingers were bleeding.

This is how it happened that one day the shuttle became stained with blood, so she dipped it in the well to wash it clean, but she let it slip and it fell in. She cried and ran to tell her stepmother what had happened, but her stepmother scolded the poor girl severely, saying, 'Since you have let the shuttle fall in, you must get it out again!'

So the girl went back, not knowing what to do, but she was so worried that at last she jumped into the well to look for the shuttle. Everything went black, and when she came to herself she was lying in a beautiful meadow, with the sun shining down on her, surrounded by thousands of wild flowers.

She stood up and walked across the meadow till she came to a baker's oven, full of bread. 'Take us out! Take us out or we shall burn!' cried the loaves. 'We have been baking quite long enough.' So she opened the oven door and pulled out all the loaves, one after another, and laid them on the grass.

On she went until she came to a tree heavily laden with ripe red apples. 'Shake us! Shake us!' cried the apples. 'We are all ripe.' So she shook the tree, and the apples fell like rain all round her. She collected them together in a heap, and continued on her way.

At last she came to a house, where she saw an old woman peering at her. She was afraid and wanted to pass by, for the old woman had great long teeth, but the old woman called to her, saying, 'What are you afraid of, my dear? Stay with me, and if you do all the housework well I will see that you are rewarded. You must take care to see that my bed is properly made, and you must give the bed-clothes a good shaking, so that the feathers fly and there is snow on the earth. I am the snow-wife.'

As the old woman seemed so kind, the girl agreed to enter her service. She worked hard and always remembered to shake the bedclothes till the feathers flew around like snowflakes. And so life passed by quite pleasantly; she was well fed, and never had to endure a single angry word.

When she had been with the snow-wife for some time,

she began to feel a little sad. At first she did not know what the matter was, but after a time she realized that she was homesick, so she went to the old woman. 'Let me go home,' she implored. 'I know I am much better off here than at home, but I have a longing to see my own folk again.'

'I am glad you want to go home,' said the snow-wife. 'You have worked hard for me, and I will show you the way back myself.' So she took her by the hand and led her to a big gateway. The gate stood open, and as the girl passed under the archway a shower of golden rain fell on her, covering her with gold from head to foot.

'That is your reward for working so hard,' said the snow-wife, and at the same time she handed her back the shuttle which had fallen into the well. The great gate closed behind her, and she found herself not far from her stepmother's house.

As she came into the yard, the cock cried out from the top of the well, 'Cock-a-doodle-doo! Our golden girl has come back to us!'

In she ran to her stepmother, and was welcomed home both by her and by her stepsister on account of the gold she had brought with her. She told them everything that had happened to her, and her stepmother wanted to procure the same good fortune for the lazy, ugly daughter. So she was made to sit by the well and spin; and in order that the shuttle might have flecks of blood on it, she stuck her hand into the hawthorn hedge and pricked her finger. Then she threw the shuttle into the well, and jumped in after it.

Like her more industrious sister, she found herself in the pleasant meadow, and she went the same way, as far

as the baker's oven. The loaves called to her, 'Take us out! Take us out or we shall burn.' But the girl shrugged her shoulders and walked on, saying, 'I don't want to make my hands dirty!'

Before long she came to the apple tree. 'Shake us! Shake us!' cried the apples. 'We are all ripe.' But she shrugged her shoulders and walked on, saying, 'Why should I shake you? You might fall on my head.'

Not long after this she reached the snow-wife's house; now she had been warned of the old woman's great long teeth, so she was not afraid, but agreed to enter her service without delay.

On the first day she made an effort to work hard and to do everything as she was told, for she was thinking of all the gold she would be given. On the second day, however, she began to grow lazy, and on the third day she was lazier still, until the time came when she simply lay in bed in the mornings and refused to get up. Nor had she any idea how to make the snow-wife's bed, and this meant that there were no feathers flying about, and no snow on the earth.

It was not very long before the snow-wife grew tired of her and sent her away, but this in no way dismayed the lazy girl, who was already thinking of the golden shower. The snow-wife took her to the gate, and as soon as she stood beneath the archway a huge pot of pitch was emptied over her. 'That is a fitting reward for your service,' said the snow-wife and shut the gate behind her.

And so the lazy girl arrived home, covered from head to foot with pitch. As she slouched past the well, the cock crowed:

'Cock-a-doodle-doo! Our dirty girl has come back to us!'

The pitch clung fast, and would not come off as long as she lived.

John Boaster

A king had a page called John Boaster, who was always making great promises which he could not keep. At the king's court there was also a jester, whose greatest delight was to make fun of John Boaster.

One day the king decided that he would like grouse for dinner, so he called John and said, 'Go out on to the hills, John, and shoot me ten grouse for my dinner.'

'Let me shoot you a hundred, Your Majesty,' said John. 'Ten will not be nearly enough!'

'All right,' said the king, 'if you are as good a shot as all that you can bring me a hundred grouse, and I will give you a shilling for each one.'

The jester overheard this conversation, and crept away out on to the hills, where he called to all the grouse:

> 'Fly away, grouse,
> make haste and take wing.
> John Boaster is coming
> to shoot for the king.'

When John came up on to the hills there was not a grouse to be seen anywhere, for they had all hidden in the heather. He had to go back to the king empty-handed, and he was put in prison for a hundred days for failing to keep his promise.

On the day after he had been set free again the king said he would like five fishes for his dinner. John remembered his hundred days in prison, and he was a little more careful. 'Your Majesty,' he said, 'permit me to catch fifty fishes for you.'

'All right,' said the king, 'if you are as good a fisherman

as all that you can bring me fifty fishes, and I will give you five shillings for each one.'

Off went the jester to the river, and called to all the fishes:

> 'Swim away, fishes,
> you'd better take care.
> John Boaster is coming
> and you must beware!'

When John came to the river he found that all the fishes had hidden under the opposite bank, where he was unable to reach them. He had to go back to the king empty-handed, and he was put in prison for fifty days for failing to keep his promise.

When the fifty days were up, the king said he would like a hare for dinner. John thought of his time in prison, and he was a little more careful still. 'Your Majesty,' he said, 'I can bring you at least ten hares.'

'All right,' said the king, 'if you are as good a huntsman

as all that, you may bring me ten hares and I will give you ten shillings for each of them.'

Away ran the jester to the fields and called to all the hares:

> 'Run away, hares,
> and hide while you may.
> John Boaster is coming
> to take you away.'

When John came out into the fields there was not a hare to be seen, and he had to go back to the king once more empty-handed. He was put in prison for ten days for not keeping his promise.

After he was released from prison, the king said he would like a roe-buck for his dinner. John thought of the long miserable days in prison that his boasting had cost him, and said modestly, 'Your Majesty, I should like to go into the woods to see if I can catch a roe-buck for you.'

So off he went and he succeeded in catching a roe-buck, which he took back to the king, feeling very pleased with himself. 'Well done!' exclaimed the king with a laugh. 'If you avoid making impossible promises you will be able to keep them!'

From that day onwards John was much more modest, and never made promises which he was unable to keep.

The Fountain

In a certain castle there once lived a young lady who was so beautiful that it would have been hard to find her equal anywhere in the world. However, she was proud, and she turned up her nose at the young men who came as suitors to the castle, even at the sons of the wealthiest noblemen.

One day along came a young man who pleased the lady greatly, and she fell in love with him, but she was too proud to confess her love. She permitted him to bring her all kinds of presents, each one more magnificent than the last, but she persisted in her refusal to become his bride.

It happened that one evening they were sitting together in a forest glade beside a spring, which came bubbling and gushing from among moss-covered rocks.

'I know that if you married me, you could bring me no princely throne as a wedding gift,' said the young lady, 'but I will consent to be your bride if you will build me a fountain in place of the thorn bushes that grow over this spring, a fountain with a great bowl set with precious stones as bright as glass and as clear as the water which will flow from it.'

Now the young man's mother was a fairy, and when he told her that evening what the young lady in the castle had demanded she built overnight a fountain whose brilliance outshone the flowers themselves.

Next morning the young lady came to him and said, 'You have done something for me, but not enough. The fountain needs a garden, and you must make me one in place of the thick forest that surrounds it: otherwise I will not be your bride.'

The young man told his mother of this new demand, and when the young lady next sat by the fountain violets and red roses sprang up around her and in the twinkling of an eye the whole forest had become a garden. Flowers covered the ground and among the bushes little birds filled the air with their singing.

This pleased the young lady immensely, and when the young man came to her she almost threw herself into his arms and promised to be his bride. But her glance fell on the castle, which now looked old and shabby and out of place beside the beautiful garden and the shimmering fountain.

'The garden is very fine,' she said, 'but there is one more thing I want from you before I become your bride. To take the place of the old castle you must build me a new one, of rubies and pearls.'

Once again the young man went to his mother, but this time the fairy grew angry. In no time the beautiful garden vanished and the bracken and brambles grew everywhere again. Only the fountain remained. There each evening the lady sits waiting and longing for her lover, but he has never come back.

Rumpelstilzkin

There was a poor miller who had a beautiful daughter. Now it happened that he had to go and speak to the king, and in order to make himself seem more important, he told the king that he had a daughter who could spin straw into gold.

'I should very much like to see how she does it,' said the king. 'Bring her to the castle tomorrow, and I will try her out.'

Next day when the girl was brought to him he took her to a room which was full of straw from floor to ceiling, and he gave her a spinning wheel, spools and a reel, saying,

'Set to work now, and if you have not spun all this straw into gold by tomorrow morning, you shall be put to death.'

With these words he closed and locked the door, and left her alone.

The poor girl was at her wits' end, for of course she had no idea how to make gold from straw, and she began to cry.

All at once, the door opened. A strange little man came in, and he said, 'Good evening to you, young lady. Why are you crying so bitterly?'

'I have to spin gold from straw,' sobbed the girl, 'and I don't know what to do!'

'What will you give me,' asked the little man, 'if I spin it for you?'

'My necklace,' replied the girl.

So the little man took the necklace and settled himself at the spinning wheel. Whirr, whirr, whirr, went the wheel, three times round, and the spool was full of gold. He changed the spool, and whirr, whirr, whirr, went the wheel, and the second spool was full. And so it went on through the night, till all the spools were full of gold, and the straw was finished.

At first light the king came in, and his eyes almost popped out of his head when he saw all the gold. He was greedy, however, and took the miller's daughter to a bigger room which had much more straw in it, and ordered her to spin it all into gold, if she valued her life.

Once again the poor girl burst into tears, and once again the door opened and the strange little man walked in.

'What will you give me,' he asked, 'if I spin all *this* straw into gold for you?'

'My ring,' she replied.

So the little man took the ring, the spinning wheel began to turn, and long before morning he had spun it all into glittering gold.

The king was delighted when he saw how much gold there was, but he wanted more still. So he took the miller's daughter to a room which was even bigger than before, and was stuffed full of straw right up to the rafters. 'You must spin all this before morning,' he said. 'If you succeed, I will marry you and you shall become queen.' For he thought that even if she was only a miller's daughter, he could hardly find a richer bride anywhere in the world.

When the girl was alone, the strange little man came to her a third time, and said, 'What will you give me this time if I spin the straw into gold?'

'I have nothing left to give you,' she replied sadly.

'Well, promise to give me your first baby when you are queen.'

'Who knows whether I shall ever be queen?' thought the miller's daughter to herself. 'But what else can I do?' So she promised the little man what he asked for, and once again he spun all the straw into gold. Next morning the king was overjoyed to see it, and he married the pretty miller's daughter, who became queen of the land.

A year later she brought a fine healthy baby into the world, but by this time she had forgotten all about the little man, until one evening the door of her room burst open and he stood before her. 'Now give me what you promised me,' he demanded.

The queen was terrified, and promised the little man all the riches of the kingdom if he would only leave her baby in peace. 'No,' said the little man, 'something living is

worth more to me than all the riches in the whole wide world!' The poor queen broke down and wept, so that the little man felt sorry for her.

'I will give you three days,' he said. 'If by the end of that time you have discovered my name, then you may keep your child.'

The queen spent the whole night trying to remember all the names that she had ever heard of, and she sent a messenger over the whole realm to make enquiries about any other names there might be in other parts of the country. Next day when the little man came, she began with John, Peter and Andrew, and went through all the names she knew, one after the other. But to each one of them the little man replied, 'No, that is not my name.'

Next day she made enquiries in the neighbourhood, and repeated all kinds of unusual and unlikely names to the little man, such as Marmaduke, Petulengro or Nebuchadnezzar. But to each of these he replied, 'No, that is not my name.'

On the third day the messenger returned to report that he had found no new names. 'But,' he said, 'as I came to a great mountain beyond the forest, where the fox and the hare were playing in the twilight, I saw a little round house, with a fire burning outside, and round the fire a strange little man hopped and danced on one leg, and he sang:

> ' "Today I sing, today I dance,
>   For I know there's not the slightest chance
>   Of saving the young queen's child from me,
>   When I go to take him as my fee
>   For no one knows, to gainsay my claim,
>   That Rumpelstilzkin is my name." '

You may imagine how overjoyed the queen was when she heard this name. That evening the little man came for the last time, saying: 'Now, Your Majesty, what is my name?'

'Is it Conrad?'

'No.'

'Is it Henry?'

'No.'

'Could it, by any chance, be Rumpelstilzkin?'

'The devil himself has told you!' shrieked the little man, and in a fury he stamped his right foot so hard on the ground that his whole leg sank into the earth. He seized his left leg with both hands, and pulled so hard that he tore himself in two.

Sungold

On the edge of a meadow, not far from a village, stood a little cottage. The people who lived there had only one child, a little girl called Sungold. She was a pretty little creature, slim as a weasel.

One sunny morning, when her mother had gone into the kitchen to get some milk, the little girl hopped out of bed and ran to the front door in her nightdress, to have a peep at the world outside. Now it was a lovely summer morning, the larks seemed to call and the flowers seemed to beckon to her, so out she went before anyone could stop her. After all, tomorrow it might be raining.

Not a moment did she waste, but ran helter-skelter across the meadow and up the hillside, into the woods. The silver birch trees were swaying gently in the breeze, and she thought she could hear them gently whispering: 'Dear me! Dear me! Whatever are you doing here? No socks, no shoes, no hat, no coat — you've nothing but your nightdress on! Dear me! Run away home again, run back do!'

She paid not the slightest attention, but ran on into the woods, and before long she came to a pond. Near the bank

was a mother duck with many ducklings, yellow as the yolk of an egg. What a cackling and squawking they started when they saw her! The mother duck flew at Sungold with her beak wide open, as if she were going to gobble her up, but Sungold was not afraid.

'Duck, you old chatterbox,' she said, 'be quiet now, so that I can look about in peace.'

'Oh, it's you, Sungold!' said the duck. 'I didn't recognize you. How are things with you? And how are your father and mother? How nice of you to come and pay us a visit! Would you like to have a look round our pond? A grand spot, isn't it?'

'Where did you find all these canaries?' asked Sungold,

when the duck had finished chattering.

'Canaries?' asked the duck. 'I beg your pardon, these are my ducklings!'

'But they sing so beautifully,' said Sungold, 'and they have no hair, but only yellow fluff! What do they feed on?'

'Clear water and fine sand.'

'They won't grow very plump on that!'

'Oh yes, they will,' said the duck. 'They find all sorts of little roots in the sand, and now and then a worm or a snail in the water.'

'Do you not have a bridge over the pond?' asked Sungold.

'No, we have no bridge,' replied the duck, 'but if you want to go over to the other side, I will gladly take you across.' So she paddled into the water, broke off a big water-lily leaf, put Sungold on it, and swam across with her to the other side of the pond, while the little fluffy yellow ducklings bobbed and squeaked along behind.

'Many thanks, Duck!' said Sungold as she stepped out on the far bank.

'Don't mention it,' said the duck. 'Just let me know if you want my help again.'

Another beautiful meadow now lay spread out before Sungold. She ran, and skipped, and danced across it, her fair hair glinting in the sunlight, and before long she came to a stork.

'Good morning, Stork,' she said. 'What is that you are eating, which croaks and is spotted green?'

'Jumping salad,' replied the stork, 'that's what it is, Sungold!'

'Give me some,' she said, 'I am hungry.'

'No, no,' said the stork, 'jumping salad is not for you.' But he prodded with his long beak in the deep water below the bank of the stream, and brought out a little golden basin full of milk, and then a roll. Then he lifted his wing, and a little paper bag full of sweets fell to the ground. Sungold ate and drank, thanked the stork for looking after her so well, and went on her way with the bag of sweets tucked into her pocket.

Before she had gone far, a blue butterfly came flying past. 'Little blue fairy,' said Sungold, 'won't you stay and play with me?'

'Delighted,' said the butterfly, 'but you mustn't touch me!'

So for a long time they played with each other, running and fluttering all over the meadow, until it began to grow dark. Then the butterfly flew away to hide in a bluebell, while Sungold sat down to rest on a patch of soft springy moss.

As she sat there she noticed that the daisies were nodding their heads sleepily. All the flowers seemed weary and ready for a night's rest, drooping and swaying in the evening breeze.

Meanwhile Sungold's poor mother was at her wits' end. She had looked all over the house for her – in all the rooms, under all the beds, in all the cupboards, and even under the stairs – but nowhere was Sungold to be found. She went up the hillside and through the woods till she came to the pond; but she was unable to cross over to the other side, so she went home, and looked again in every nook and cranny. The more she looked, the more she cried. And all this time Sungold's father was looking all over the village, and asking everyone he met if they had seen her.

Now there are twelve angels, who fly all over the whole world every night, just to make sure that no little boy or girl has been left out or has got lost. When it was quite dark, one of these angels flew over the green meadow, and he saw Sungold, who now lay asleep in the grass. Gently he raised the sleeping child in his arms and flew back with her to her parents' house. Quietly he laid her under the stairs, and flew away.

Her father was sitting miserably at the table, while her mother, carrying a candle, was having one last look all over the house, sobbing as if her heart would break. When she looked under the stairs, Sungold's fair hair gleamed in the candle-light. Her mother cried out for joy and quick as a flash her husband was beside her under the stairs, and they stood looking down on the sleeping child. 'Where was she?' the man asked. 'She was asleep under the stairs, and I have looked there so often already!' said the mother.

The man shook his head. 'There's something strange about this,' he said. 'But let us thank God that our little Sungold has come back to us.'

The Hair from the Queen of the Underworld

Three brothers left home together in search of adventure. One day they came to a great hole in the ground, which led into the underworld.

The two older ones said to the youngest one, 'We are going to tie you up, and drop you into the hole so that you can see what there is down there.'

He tried to run away, but they tied him up with their belts and dropped him into the hole. He fell into a house belonging to an old sorceress.

'What do you want here?' asked the old woman.

'I have been sent by the King of the Upperworld, to fetch him a hair from the head of the Queen of the Underworld.'

'How do you propose to do that, my lad?' she asked. 'She is guarded by a terrible dog with three heads, who sleeps neither night nor day.'

'How do you think I should do it?' he asked.

'Take this water,' she replied, 'and when you reach her dwelling wash your face in it, so that you will turn invisible and the dog will not be able to see you. Go in then, and if the Queen of the Underworld is sleeping you must drop a little of this earth into her ear, so that she will not hear you. Then you must pull a golden hair out of her head and come back as fast as you can.'

He did as he had been told, and washed his face in the magic water, so that he became invisible and the dog could not see him. Then he went in and found the Queen of the Underworld asleep, so he poured a little of the magic earth into her ear, and she heard nothing. Quickly he pulled a golden hair out of her head, and returned to the old sorceress.

'What are you going to do now?' she asked.

'I want to go up to the Upperworld again,' he replied. 'How do you think I should do it?'

The old woman called all the crows together, and tied a piece of meat to his waist. The crows began to pull and tug at the meat, and as they tugged, they pulled him higher and higher, till at last he could climb out into the Upperworld.

His brothers were amazed to see him again. He took the golden hair to the King, who gave him a great deal of money for it; for whoever holds the hair in his hand shines like the sun. So he became one of the richest men in the world, and his two brothers had to serve him.

The Man in the Moon

One fine Sunday morning many years ago a man went into the forest. He felled a tree, chopped up the wood, tied it into a bundle, lifted it on to his shoulder, and set off for home. On the way he met a young man dressed in his best clothes, who was on the way to church.

'Do you not know,' asked the man, 'that today is the day of rest on earth? God rested on the seventh day after he had made the world and all the creatures in it. Do you not know the third commandment, where it is written: "Remember the Sabbath day, to keep it holy"?'

The young man who spoke was God himself in disguise. But the wood-cutter answered rudely, 'Sunday, Monday, all days are the same to me!'

God said, 'Then you shall carry your bundle of firewood for ever, and you shall live in the moon, as a warning to all who will not keep the Sabbath holy.'

From that day to this there has always been a man in

the moon with a bundle of wood on his shoulder, and he will be there for ever and ever.

The Wild Swans

There was once a farmer who lived with his wife and their young daughter and baby son. One day the parents went to market, and the mother said to her daughter, 'We will bring you back some cakes, and a new apron. Be good: take care of your baby brother and do not go out of the house.'

But as soon as they had gone the girl forgot what she had been told. She laid her baby brother down in the grass, and went out to play in the road.

The wild swans flew over, and they spied the little boy on the ground. They swooped down and carried him off.

When the girl came home she found that her baby brother had gone. She searched and called for him, but there was no sign of him anywhere. She ran out into the fields. Far, far in the distance the wild swans were flying away, and she saw them disappear behind the dark forest.

She guessed that it was the swans who had stolen her baby brother, so she ran after them. On and on she ran, till she came to a baker's oven that stood beside the track.

'Oven, dear oven, where have the swans flown?'

'First eat my rye bread,' replied the oven, 'and then I will tell you.'

'But at home we have only fine wheaten bread!' she said.

The oven answered not a word.

On she ran, till she came to a wild apple tree.

'Apple tree, dear apple tree,' said the girl, 'tell me where the wild swans have flown.'

'First eat my green apples,' replied the apple tree, 'and I will tell you.'

'But at home we have only red apples!' she said. The apple tree answered not a word.

On she ran, till she came to a river of milk, whose banks were made of porridge.

'River, dear river,' she said, 'where have the wild swans flown?'

'First drink my milk and eat my porridge,' replied the river, 'and then I will tell you.'

'But at home we have only *cream* with our porridge,' she said. The river answered not a word.

For a long, long time the girl ran on through the forest and over the fields, till she stumbled over a hedgehog. She would have pushed it out of her way, but she was afraid of pricking herself, so instead she asked him, 'Hedgehog, dear hedgehog, did *you* see which way the wild swans flew?'

'Look over there!' he replied, pointing with his sharp little black nose.

The girl ran where he had pointed, and there she found a little hut standing on hens' legs and feet, turning slowly round and round. Inside the hut she could see the old witch Spindleshanks, but on a bench by the window sat her baby brother, playing with golden apples.

Without making a sound she crept up to the window, took her brother in her arms, and ran away with him.

Before long, however, the wild swans were on her track, and she could hear their beating wings drawing nearer.

Where could she hide? There lay the river of milk in front of her.

'River, dear river,' she implored, 'hide me!'

'First drink my milk and eat my porridge,' said the river.

There was nothing else for it, so she ate the porridge with milk, and the river hid her beneath its banks. The wild swans flew overhead.

'Thank you very much,' she said, as she crawled out again, and continued on her way with her baby brother in her arms. But the wild swans had swung round, and before long they were flying straight towards her. What could she do? There stood the wild apple tree just in front of her.

'Apple tree, dear apple tree,' she said, 'please, will you hide me?'

'First eat my green apples,' replied the apple tree.

Quickly she ate the apples, and the tree lowered its branches and covered her with its leaves. The wild swans flew overhead.

On she ran with her baby brother, but the wild swans spied her and turned again. Soon they would reach her, and snatch her brother back. There, fortunately, stood the baker's oven.

'Oven, dear oven, *please* hide me!' she implored.

'First eat my rye bread,' replied the oven.

So she swallowed the bread without wasting a moment, and thrust herself and her baby brother into the oven. The wild swans beat their wings outside, and screamed with rage, but they could not reach her. At last they flew away.

The girl ran quickly home with her brother, and luckily she reached the house just before her parents arrived back.

The King of the Cats

One cold winter evening a grave-digger's wife sat by the fire, waiting for her husband to come home. Her big black cat, old Tom, lay blinking sleepily, curled up on the bench beside her. They waited and waited, but there was no sign of the husband.

When at last he came, he rushed in out of breath and very upset. 'Who is Tommy Tildrum?' he asked. His wife and the cat gaped at him.

'What is the matter with you?' asked his wife. 'Why do you want to know who Tommy Tildrum is?'

'You can have no idea what I have seen!' replied the man. 'I had finished digging old Mr Fordyce's grave, and I must have fallen asleep beside it, for I was woken by the cry of a cat.'

'Miaow!' said old Tom.

'Yes, just like that,' said the man. 'I looked over the grave, and what do you think I saw?'

'How should I know?' said his wife.

'Just imagine: nine black cats, just like Tom, each with a white patch on his chest. And what do you think they were carrying? A small coffin, covered with a black velvet cloth, and on top of the cloth lay a golden crown. And every third step all the cats cried "Miaow!"'

'Miaow!' repeated old Tom.

'Yes, just like that,' said the grave-digger. 'And as they came nearer and nearer, their eyes glowed green out of the darkness. They were coming straight towards me. Eight of them were carrying the coffin, and the ninth marched in front, slowly and full of dignity – but just look at our Tom – see how he is staring at me! You would think he

understands every word I say!'

'Carry on, carry on!' said his wife. 'Don't trouble yourself about old Tom.'

'Well, on they came towards me, slowly and solemnly, and at every third step they cried "Miaow!"'

'Miaow!' repeated old Tom.

The grave-digger looked at Tom in surprise, and turned pale. But he went on: 'Just think, they all lined up along the far edge of the grave, and stood there looking across at me with their great green eyes – but just look at Tom! He is looking at me exactly as they did!'

'Carry on, carry on!' said his wife. 'Don't worry yourself about the old cat!'

'Well, where was I? Oh yes, they were all standing staring at me. Then the cat who was not helping to carry the coffin came round to my side of the grave, looked me straight in the face, and said to me, in a voice which was squeaky but quite clear, "Tell Tom Tildrum that Tim Toldrum is dead." Well, I ask you, how on earth should I know who Tom Tildrum is? And how in the world can

I tell Tom Tildrum that Tim Toldrum is dead if I don't know who Tom Tildrum is?'

'Look at old Tom, look at old Tom!' shrieked the woman.

The grave-digger gave a start. Old Tom jumped to the floor. He puffed himself out, arched his back, and screamed, 'What, is old Tim dead? Then I am King of the Cats!'

With these words the old cat shot up the chimney and was never seen again.

Little Johnny

There was once a little fellow called Johnny, who slept all night long in a cot upon wheels, and in the afternoons too, if he was tired. But when he was not tired (which happened quite often) his mother had to push him round the room, and he could never have enough of this.

Now one night little Johnny lay awake in his cot upon wheels. His mother was asleep in her great fourposter bed beside him.

'Mummy,' cried little Johnny, 'push me round the room!'

Sleepily his mother stretched out an arm and began to push the cot backwards and forwards. When her arm grew tired and the rolling grew slower, Johnny called out, 'More! More!' Then the rolling began again, backwards and forwards, to and fro, till at last she fell asleep again; and no matter how loud Johnny cried, she paid no attention to him.

Before long the old moon peeped through the window to see what was going on, and what he saw was so comical that he had to rub his eyes to make sure that he was not imagining it. Such a thing he had never seen in all his days!

For there lay little Johnny with his eyes wide open, and one leg stuck up into the air just like the mast of a ship. He had taken off his little nightdress, and tucked the tip of it between his toes. Then he took the other end of the nightdress in his two hands, so that it was like a sail, and he puffed out his cheeks and blew.

And gradually, very softly, very slowly, the cot began to roll. It rolled across the floor, up the wall, across the ceiling, and down the other wall, till it came back to where it had started.

'More! More!' cried Johnny. And he puffed out his cheeks again, and went up the wall and across the ceiling once more.

After he had repeated the journey three times, the moon suddenly peered into his face and said, 'Little fellow, have you not had enough yet?'

'Not at all,' cried Johnny, 'more, more! Open the door and let me out! I must roll through the town, and every-one must see me as I go.'

'I can't open the door,' said the kind old moon, but he sent a moonbeam through the keyhole, and little Johnny rolled along it out into the streets.

But the streets were quite empty and he was lonely there. The tall houses towered up in the moonlight, and glowered down on him with their great dark windows. Not a soul was to be seen. What a rattling and clattering there was, as little Johnny trundled in his cot over the cobbled streets and squares! The good old moon stayed with him in order to light the way, and on they went, up and down and in and out, till they had been through the whole town, but still not a soul did they see.

As they passed the church tower, the golden cock on top of it crowed, 'Cock-a-doodle-doo!' They stopped to look at it. 'What are you doing up there?' called little Johnny.

'That was my first call,' shouted the cock, craning his neck to see who was out and about at this early hour in the morning. 'When I crow for the third time, then it is time for people to wake up.'

'I can't wait all that time,' said Johnny. 'I must go into the forest, and all the creatures must see me as I go!'

'Have you not had enough yet, little fellow?' asked the moon.

'No,' cried Johnny, 'more, more! Light the way, old moon!' And he puffed out his chest and blew, and the good old moon lit the way, and they came through the city gates and across the open country into the dark woods. The trees were so close together that the moon could hardly pass between them. At one point he was left quite a long way behind, but he managed to catch up with Johnny in a clearing.

Everything was silent, not a leaf stirred, and there were no animals to be seen – not a roebuck, not a hare, not even a little mouse. On and on they went, through pine-woods and beech-woods, birch-woods and oak-woods, and the good old moon lit the way wherever they went.

The only living creature which they saw was a tiny kitten sitting in the fork of an oak tree, its eyes glowing in the darkness. They stopped to look. 'That is little Tibbie,' said Johnny. 'I know her well. She is trying to shine like the stars.'

Johnny trundled past, the little kitten ran overhead, leaping from branch to branch and from tree to tree, trying to keep level with them. 'What are you doing up there?' called Johnny.

'I am lighting the way for you!' replied Tibbie.

'Where are all the other animals?' asked Johnny.

'They are all asleep,' replied Tibbie, as she sprang across a gap to another tree. 'Just listen to them snoring!'

'Little fellow,' said the good old moon, 'have you not had enough yet?'

'Not at all,' cried Johnny, 'more, more! Keep shining, old moon!' And he puffed out his cheeks, and on he rolled faster than ever, so that he soon left Tibbie the kitten far behind. Before long they rolled out of the wood and up a slope to the end of the world, and then they just flew on into the sky.

This was much better fun! The stars were all awake, and sparkled and twinkled all around them. 'Make way there!' cried Johnny, as he flew faster than ever through the bright crowd, sending stars scurrying in all directions, so that some of them fell right out of the sky.

'Have you not had enough yet, little fellow?' asked the moon.

'No,' said Johnny, 'faster, faster!' And he rolled right across the moon's face, leaving a brown streak behind him.

This was too much for the poor old moon, who sneezed three times and put out his light. One after the other the stars went out, and it was soon so dark in the sky that you could almost break off pieces of darkness in your hands.

185

'Light up, old moon, light up!' cried Johnny.

But neither moon nor stars were anywhere to be seen, for they had all gone to bed. Then Johnny grew frightened when he found himself alone in the great vault of the sky. He clasped the corners of his nightdress more tightly than ever, and blew with might and main, but he had no idea where he was going, and he went zig-zagging all over the sky. No one saw him go, not even the stars.

At last he looked down and saw a great round red face looking up at him from the edge of the sky, and he thought this was the good old moon once more. 'Light up, old moon!' he cried. And he sailed across the sky towards it, only to find that it was the sun just rising out of the sea.

'Young fellow,' growled the sun, as he glared at him with his huge blazing eyes, 'what are you doing here in

my sky?' And he gripped little Johnny by the scruff of the neck and hurled him down into the sea.

What happened then?

Well, don't you know? Little Johnny had never learnt to swim, so he would certainly have drowned if you and I had not come along in our boat and rescued him!

Some other Young Puffins

LUCKY DIP *Ruth Ainsworth*

Stories from the BBC's *Listen With Mother*. Seven of the ever-popular *Charles* stories are included. (Also available in Initial Teaching Alphabet edition)

THE TEN TALES OF SHELLOVER *Ruth Ainsworth* *

The Black Hens, the Dog and the Cat didn't like Shellover the tortoise at first, until they discovered what wonderful stories he told.

LITTLE PETE STORIES *Leila Berg* †

More favourites from *Listen With Mother*, about a small boy who plays mostly by himself. Illustrated by Peggy Fortnum.

A BEAR CALLED PADDINGTON *Michael Bond* *

MORE ABOUT PADDINGTON *

PADDINGTON HELPS OUT *

PADDINGTON AT LARGE *

PADDINGTON AT WORK *

PADDINGTON ABROAD *

PADDINGTON MARCHES ON *

Named after the railway station on which he was found, Paddington is an intelligent, well-meaning, likeable bear who somehow always manages to get into trouble. Illustrated by Peggy Fortnum.

THE CASTLE OF YEW *Lucy M. Boston*

Joseph visits the magic garden where the yew trees are shaped like castles – and finds himself shrunk small enough to crawl inside one.

* *Not available for sale in the U.S.A.*
† *Not available for sale in the U.S.A. or Canada*

THE HAPPY ORPHELINE *Natalie Savage Carlson* †

The twenty little orphaned girls who lived with Madame Flattot are terrified of being adopted because they are so happy.

A BROTHER FOR THE ORPHELINES †

Natalie Savage Carlson

Josine, the smallest of the orphans, finds a baby boy left on the doorstep and the orphans plot and worry to find a way to keep him.

FIVE DOLLS IN A HOUSE *Helen Clare*

A little girl called Elizabeth finds a way of making herself small and visits her dolls in their own house.

TELL ME A STORY *Eileen Colwell*

TELL ME ANOTHER STORY

TIME FOR A STORY

Stories, verses, and finger plays for children of 3 to 6, collected by the greatest living expert on the art of children's story-telling.

MY NAUGHTY LITTLE SISTER *Dorothy Edwards* †

MY NAUGHTY LITTLE SISTER'S FRIENDS †

These now famous stories were originally told by a mother to her own children. Ideal for reading aloud. For ages 4 to 8.

MISS HAPPINESS AND MISS FLOWER *Rumer Godden* *

Nona was lonely far away from her home in India, and the two dainty Japanese dolls, Miss Happiness and Miss Flower, were lonely too. But once Nona started building them a proper Japanese house they all felt happier. Illustrated by Jean Primrose.

THREE LITTLE FUNNY ONES *Charlotte Hough*

Oliver, Timmy and Tom have some adventures which are just frightening enough to make them interesting, like when they make a lion trap and catch a sausage dog. (Also available in Initial Teaching Alphabet.)

* Not Available for Sale in the U.S.A.
† Not Available for Sale in the U.S.A. or Canada

MY AUNT'S ALPHABET *Charlotte Hough*

A gay and colourful alphabet with a word and picture appeal which no young child (reader or non-reader) will be able to resist. (*A Young Puffin Original.*)

THE STORY OF FERDINAND *Munro Leaf* †

The endearing story of the adventures of the nicest bull there ever was – and it has a very happy ending.

MEET MARY KATE *Helen Morgan* *

Charmingly told stories of a four-year-old's everyday life in the country. Illustrated by Shirley Hughes.

PUFFIN BOOK OF NURSERY RHYMES
Peter and Iona Opie

The first comprehensive collection of nursery rhymes to be produced as a paperback, prepared for Puffins by the leading authorities on children's lore. 220 pages, exquisitely illustrated on every page by Pauline Baynes. (*A Young Puffin Original.*)

LITTLE OLD MRS PEPPERPOT *Alf Prøysen* *
MRS PEPPERPOT TO THE RESCUE *

Gay little stories about an old woman who suddenly shrinks to the size of a pepperpot.

ROM-BOM-BOM AND OTHER STORIES *Antonia Ridge*

A collection of animal stories written by the distinguished children's author and broadcaster. For 4 to 8 year olds.

DEAR TEDDY ROBINSON *Joan G. Robinson*

Teddy Robinson was Deborah's teddy bear and such a very nice, friendly cuddly bear that he went everywhere with her and had even more adventures than she did.

* *Not Available for Sale in the U.S.A.*
† *Not Available for Sale in the U.S.A. or Canada*

THE ADVENTURES OF GALLDORA *Modwena Sedgwick*

This lovable rag doll belonged to Marybell, who wasn't always very careful to look after her, so Galldora was always getting lost – in a field with a scarecrow, on top of a roof, and in all sorts of other strange places.

SOMETHING TO DO *Septima*

Suggestions for games to play and things to make and do each month, from January to December. It is designed to help mothers with young children at home. (*A Young Puffin Original*)

PONDER AND WILLIAM *Barbara Softly*
PONDER AND WILLIAM ON HOLIDAY

Ponder the panda looks after William's pyjamas and is a wonderful companion in these all the year round adventures. Illustrated by Diana John. (*A young Puffin Original*)

CLEVER POLLY AND THE STUPID WOLF
Catherine Storr

Clever Polly manages to think of lots of good ideas to stop the stupid wolf from eating her.

DANNY FOX *David Thomson*

Clever Danny Fox helps the Princess to marry the fisherman she loves and comes safely home to his hungry family. (*A Young Puffin Original*)

DANNY FOX MEETS A STRANGER *David Thomson*

The stranger was a big grey wolf, and he was out to steal Danny's den and hunting grounds. (*A Young Puffin Original*)

THE URCHIN *Edith Unnerstad* *

The Urchin is only five years old – but already he has the Larsson family at sixes and sevens with his ingenious tricks and adventures.

LITTLE O *Edith Unnerstad* *

The enchanting story of the youngest of the Pip Larsson family.

* Not available for sale in the U.S.A.